CRIPPLE

THE FIRST BROKEN BOOK

A 21st CENTURY PARABLE BY NICK MAYNARD

Published by New Generation Publishing in 2020

Copyright © Nick Maynard 2020

First Edition

The author asserts the moral right under the Copyright, Designs and Patents Act 1988 to be identified as the author of this work.

All Rights reserved. No part of this publication may be reproduced, stored in a retrieval system or transmitted, in any form or by any means without the prior consent of the author, nor be otherwise circulated in any form of binding or cover other than that which it is published and without a similar condition being imposed on the subsequent purchaser.

ISBN
  Paperback 978-1-80031-888-5
  Ebook 978-1-80031-887-8

www.newgeneration-publishing.com

WHAT'S YOUR STORY?

This book was shortlisted in the Pen to Print Book Challenge Competition and has been produced by
The London Borough of Barking and Dagenham Library Service - Pen to Print Creative Writing Programme. This is supported with National Portfolio Organisation funding from Arts Council, England.

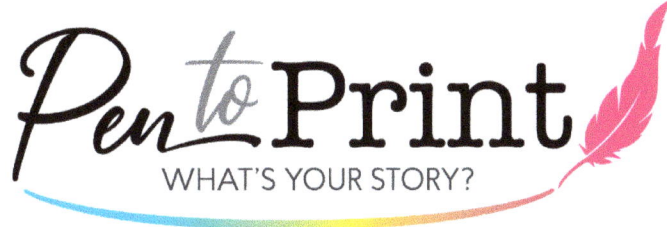

Connect with Pen to Print
Email: pentoprint@lbbd.gov.uk
Web: pentoprint.org

vade mecum

I would like to thank *The Book Challenge* and *The London Borough of Barking and Dagenham's Pen to Print Project* for all their support and belief in me, and to the judges, for giving me this opportunity, after so many others wouldn't. And to Anna Robinson, who has mentored me through this process, for all her patience and wisdom. And to everyone who said I could, even if they thought I couldn't.

E.V.A.[1]

This book is dedicated to three special people:

> My nan, who gave me her love of words, and taught me more than she would ever know. My mum, who left school hardly being able to read or write properly – and taught herself so that she could read me stories at night. And Andi – whom I love without condition, in this world and the rest.

---

[1] Eva – the name in Hebrew means *'life'*.

I know I hung a windswept tree,
Nine long days and nights.
Gashed by mine-own spear,
Sacrificed to Odin,
An offering to myself.
Bound to a tree that no man knows,
        whither its roots do run.

None gave me bread,
Nor gave me ale.
And I peered down into the deepest depths,
        and there I saw the runes,
With a mighty cry I seized them up
        and fell back into myself once again.

As I won back my strength, wisdom thrived too,
As word leads to word, and deed to deed.
I understood my course.

***Havamal**[2] - The Poetic Edda, c 1200 AD.*

---

[2] For the poem's annotation and meaning. *See* Notes.

CRIPPLE

THE FIRST BROKEN BOOK

A 21st CENTURY PARABLE

TEXT AND PICTURES BY NICK MAYNARD

CONTENTS

Prologue: The Hanged Man 1

Book One - The Hermit's Book
FREYA'S AETTIR
Father, Birth and the Body

Chapter One - Possession 3
Chapter Two - Strength 11
Chapter Three - Gateway 20
Chapter Four - Signals 29
Chapter Five - Journey 36
Chapter Six - Opening 42
Chapter Seven - Gift 48
Chapter Eight - Joy 53

Book Two - The Lover's Book
HAGAL'S AETTIR
The Son, Growth and the Mind

Chapter One - Disruption 60
Chapter Two - Need 74
Chapter Three - Standstill 84
Chapter Four - Year 89
Chapter Five - Defence 98
Chapter Six - Initiation 108
Chapter Seven - Protector 111
Chapter Eight - Wholeness 118

Book Three - The Mortal's Book
TIR'S AETTIR
The Soul, Death and the Holy Spirit

Chapter One - Warrior 121
Chapter Two - Growth 138
Chapter Three - Movement 150
Chapter Four - Self 158

Chapter Five - Flow 164
Chapter Six - People 171
Chapter Seven - Separation 181
Chapter Eight – Day 184
Chapter Nine - Unknown 193

APPENDIX

Appendix I: Odin 195
Appendix II: The Runes 197
Appendix III: Collective Consciousness 206
Appendix IV: Michelangelo 209
Appendix V: The Alexander Technique 211
Appendix VI: Astral Projection 213
Appendix VII: Dream Magic 219
Appendix VIII: Dionysus 222
Appendix IX: Ecstasy 226
Appendix X: Ketamine 228
Appendix XI: *The Bible* in Context 230

NOTES

A New Age of Machines 235
Aleister Crowley 238
Osiris 244
Horus the Sun 246
The Annotated *'Havamal'* 248

Further Crippled 250

Conclusion 257

Prologue: The Hanged Man

The Hanged Man[3] accepts his fate. The self-sacrifice he makes is rewarded, for as he dies, he is re-born.[4] He is suspended[5] between two worlds,[6] the material[7] and ethereal,[8] and in sacrificing himself[9] 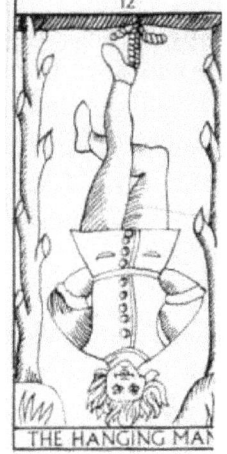 he understands all.[10] His willing sacrifice bringing forth wisdom and intuition, release and divination.[11]

***

The man is suspended in space, his physical isolation reflecting his emotional loneliness. The uncomfortable position of his body mirrors his inner personal torment. Yet, on his face there is no demonstration of pain,[12] as he – like many of us – does not see his own confusion, or the chaos of the world beyond him.

---

[3] The Tarot deck depicts this card as a man who hangs upside down, by his right foot, from a cross beam balanced between two trees, his hands tied behind his back.

[4] Linked to the death and resurrection of the ancient Egyptian god Osiris, the Norse god Odin and the Christian deity Jesus Christ.

[5] Suspended is, of course, another word for 'hanging' and the word 'man' derives its meaning from the Sanskrit root word for 'mind'. Thus 'Hanging Man' can be seen, esoterically, as symbolising 'the suspended mind'.

[6] Symbolised by the two trees.

[7] The physical world in which we live.

[8] The spiritual world beyond the realms of the 'physical' world.

[9] The Self can be seen as 'I' or 'The Ego'. That part of us which is conscious of ourselves and therefore represents the individual.

[10] In this case, 'all' represents 'universal consciousness', a term given to a 'collective consciousness' which goes beyond the individual consciousness of The Self. This 'collective' awareness can be seen in our almost instinctive responses to things beyond our own experience. In essence, it is the thought that links humanity. (See Appendix III)

[11] The traditional interpretation of the twelfth card of the Tarot's Major Arcana (which comprises of 22 allegorical cards), which is better known as The Hanged Man.

[12] In the Marseille Tarot pack The Hanged Man is smiling.

The man's head and arms form the shape of an inverted triangle, his head – the apex – pointing downwards, representing turmoil,[13] his legs crossed, denoting the physical world[14] weighing down upon him.

Sometimes the man is seen as Judas Iscariot, the disciple who betrayed Christ[15] for thirteen pieces of silver.[16] Often seen as a negative action, but without Judas' betrayal there would have been no crucifixion, no resurrection and no redemption. Without Judas there would have been no salvation of mankind and subsequently no Christian Church. Quite simply, without Judas' betrayal of Jesus, Jesus would not have fulfilled his destiny by sacrificing himself upon the cross.

The Hanged Man is also graphically opposite to the Tarot card called The World,[17] which shows a woman standing, with her head and hands arranged in the familiar posture of a triangle, her feet crossed as if in dance. Unlike The Hanged Man, this card represents freedom and inner peace.

The Hanged Man also symbolises Odin[18] the crippled god, with the power of second-sight, and the keeper of the secrets of the runes.[19]

---

[13] It is also interesting to note that in the Nazi Concentration Camps homosexual prisoners were identified by a pink inverted triangle stitched to their prison uniforms. Pink has often been associated with reconciliation and harmony. Although it is more likely the colour was chosen as a means of ridicule, as it is a colour traditionally associated with femininity. It is also important to note that the Judas Tree blossoms in spring and that the bloom is pink in colour.

[14] The Cross points to the four elements of the physical world – earth, air, water and fire.

[15] With a kiss.

[16] In some Tarot decks The Hanged Man is depicted holding two bags of silver.

[17] Which is number 21 in the deck (note: The Hanged Man is number 12).

[18] *See* Appendix I.

[19] *See* Appendix II.

BOOK ONE
The Hermit's Book

FREYA'S AETTIR[20]

Father, Birth and the Body.

Chapter One - Possession

12.30 p.m.   Thursday, 8th May 2003.

A boy's bedroom in suburbia!
Suburbia.[21] A state of mind rather than a real place.[22] An enclave of twitching curtains and carefully tended lawns.[23]

---

[20] Freya's Aettir (*Freya - Feoh* or *Fehu*) is the first of three sets of eight runes (twenty-four in all) used in divination or fortune telling. (*See* Appendix II)

This bedroom – a teenage boy's headroom...

The walls are full of faded football posters – a pin-board is crammed with curling photographs.[24]

One face is predominant. The pictures of a boy – a handsome young man – his image burnt into the two-dimensional shape of a photograph. A glossy card to be locked away and forgotten about until found.

This photograph collects dust now – jailed in time. No names. They don't matter here anymore. Their duty now is to stand as a shrine – a freak's museum that cries an uneasy, discomforting cry. In the stale air of this room you can almost hear these frozen moments. Their vivid world is blending into the here and now. Face-to-face with the past.

You could almost touch it. As though you could gaze into those bright, big eyes without the gloss between you.

But who is this boy? The tenant of the room.

***

A young man, in his twenties,[25] sits – he is confined to a wheelchair.

This was once his room. These were once his possessions. Now it is he who is possessed; curling like the photographs and fading like the posters.

---

[21] In this street it meant a place where people spend money they don't have, on things they don't need, to impress people they don't like.

[22] Seeing as by the time you've paid off the mortgage the suburbs have moved 10 miles further out.

[23] Where children are genetically programmed to match the furniture.

[24] Just passed-over pieces of a life – a time-capsule of a young existence, which stopped – seven years ago.

[25] The boy's name is Jonathan (from the Hebrew meaning 'the Lord has given'). Born on Wednesday, 11th June, 1980 (under the sun-sign Gemini).

He is a quadriplegic, [26] twisted and wasted.

***

Birthdays, Christmas... Half remembered holidays by the sea. Not liking the feeling of sand between his toes or it sticking to his fingers. What he would give to have that sensation again. Now the episodes of his life flash by him at a hundred mile an hour. Edited in his mind like a badly made Super-8.[27] The frames sometimes dark and obscured, as though he's out of focus and fuzzy, with fragments sometimes underexposed, and moments missing.

Scratchy.

Sepia.

Silent.

Night!

***

And what of his life? Was there anything there in his past to redeem him? He was fifteen. He hasn't lived long enough for that. At that age life is all about sensation. Frustration... Redemption comes later.

It was a Friday night.[28] Suffolk was hotter than Miami.[29] And his hormones were raging. It was just the right cocktail of ingredients for a house party to celebrate the start of the Summer Holidays.

Jonathan (*aka* Jonny, to his friends) had spent an hour in the bathroom showering, deodorising, and pulling faces in the mirror. He'd gelled his hair, squeezed his spot and thrown a tantrum at not

---

[26] A person with paralysis of all four limbs.
[27] A name given to the film stock used in home-movies before the advent of video and digital cameras.
[28] Friday, 21st July, 1995.
[29] 32 degrees. But this was Manchester, and just as hot.

being able to find *'the shirt'* that lived at the bottom of the wash-basket. By 9 o'clock he was ready.

His dad had offered to drive him, so he took the bus! A quick detour into the off-licence and he was there, at Julia's house.

Julia's parents had gone away for the weekend and she, and her sister,[30] were having the first party of the summer.

The house was a 'semi'[31] filled with music,[32] teenagers and the mingling sounds of a thousand stories. The tale of Julia and Ste.[33] The ballad of Chris and Debbie.[34] And, of course, the comic interludes of Becky, Sonia and Janine, who sit on the stairs, get pissed and cry alternately.

But what was Jonathan's story?

***

Here he was well groomed and well presented, with a cheeky smile, and the sort of credentials you would be stupid to ignore.[35] He lived in the right part of town, wore the right sort of clothes, from the right sort of shops, and he confident. He was smooth, he was assured – and he was single.

So, what was his story?

He'd just split up with his girlfriend of four months,[36] and was 'on the pull' for another one. Same sort of model, but maybe with more leg-room and some added extras. And this was the showroom. Small ones, tall ones – some as big as your mum... All he had to do was

---

[30] Who was called Wendy and was studying history at York University.
[31] Semi-detached house.
[32] Blur's *Park Life*.
[33] Julie and Ste had been seeing each other for nearly a year.
[34] Chris had 'got off' with a girl called Zoe the weekend before, and Debbie had just found out.
[35] He was captain of the school football team.
[36] Lisa Taylor was blonde, with blue-eyes and an ample bosom.

choose. And that's the way he strolled into the party as he surveyed the quarry.

An attractive girl was sat by the neat, little stacking-system, blasting out Oasis' *Roll with It* - so Jonathan took heed from the song and did. The girl smiled at him and he moved into another room. The kitchen had brighter light and everyone was talking drunken bollocks, so he quickly noted 'the talent' and headed upstairs.

He negotiated his way through the fat girls sat on the stairs, and went into Julia's bedroom.

He knew where her room was, because before she'd met Ste, they'd had 'a thing' together. It hadn't been anything serious. They were only thirteen. But he did get to see the inside of her room – if you know what I mean.

Jonathan saw the girl by the stacking-system was his 'safety' and the girls in the kitchen as his 'possibles', if he got desperate.

Jonny *(as he approached her)* Mind if I sit here?

She registered him with a smile, moved along the bed – to give him space... Just enough... She smoothed down her clothes, to allow him her best presentation.

The girl with no name   You're Jonny, aren't you?

His reputation went before him.

The girl with no name   I'm...

He didn't catch the name, and he didn't much care. This was easy. Too easy! Did he want her? Of course he did.

Jonny   You a friend of Julia's then?

The girl with no name   Ye'. And you?

Jonny   We used to go out together… Before her and Ste.

She just nodded and thought of something else to say, as he took a swig from his can of Carling. Too easy.

The girl with no name   You not going out with that girl no more?

Jonny   Lisa? No, we split up.

The girl with no name   What happened?

He just shrugged and pulled a face. It was the wrong question and she scoured her memory-banks for something better to say.

The girl with no name   Plenty more fish in the sea, aye?

And that was the best she could come up with? Jonny took another gulp from his can.

Jonny   Drink?

He offers the can, and she accepts.

The girl with no name   Thanks.

As the can is passed back, the moment is set. He reads her eyes. Her lips still slightly parted. He moves towards her. She moves towards him. And they kiss. A long, dirty kiss. The sort of kiss you have when you're a teenager. The sort that last for as long as you have air in your lungs. The sort that gives a fifteen-year-old boy a hard-on.

***

The young man's thoughts snap back into the here and now, as his mother[37] disturbs his silence with a bowl of chicken broth.

---

[37] Mothers are people who can look in a drawer and find a pair of socks that aren't there.

Mother   Watching the world go by, are we?[38] Ready for your lunch? Let's put this over your shirt, so you don't spill.

She puts a tea-towel around his neck, infantilising him.

Mother   There we go. Open nice and wide for Mummy.

But it doesn't matter. Her words are wasted. He doesn't hear. He doesn't know.

Mother   We're spilling.

She scrapes the spilt food from around his mouth with the spoon. And as she shovels, she speaks.

Mother   Is that good? Could you hear the bird's singing this morning? They've made a nest right outside my bedroom window. Ooo, they do make a noise. Cherp! Cherp! Cherp! They've been going all morning. I don't know how they have the energy. Is that nice? Want some more?

She loads another spoonful and tips it carefully into her offspring's twisted mouth. She doesn't see her boy anymore. He's just become an extension of the dusting and bed-making of everyday life.

Mother   Open wide like a good boy. That's it. One more and then we're done. That's a good boy. Was that nice?

She starts to clean him up with the tea-towel.

Mother   That big, bad Magpie came back again this morning. The other birds won't eat while he's there.[39] I think

---

[38] She's stopped waiting for him to answer.
[39] They say the Magpie is The Devil Bird, and carries a drop of his master's blood under his tongue. He was the only animal not to attend the Crucifixion in full mourning dress – 'One for sorrow, two for joy, three for a letter, four for a boy,

he frightens them. Ooo, he's a messy eater. Ugly thing he is. You should see him. He doesn't leave anything for the other birds. The other day I put out nearly a full loaf and he'd have eaten the lot if I hadn't have gone out and shooed him off. There! All clean again.

She resents the mess. A house-proud mother, who'd smack his legs for having dirty knees, if things had been different.

Mother   Mummy's got some jobs to do now, but I'll be back up again as soon as I've finished. You'll be all right on your own, won't you? Of course you will. You're a big boy now, aren't you? See all those dickey-birds? Aren't they funny? See you in a little while.

Click!

And the door shuts behind her, and she is gone. The faint sound of her retreat – and then nothing. It's as though she'd never been there. Her disruption lasting only a few moments.

The window is his only friend.

And in his head, he speaks.

I am alive. And as long as I remember that I won't die.

And then the warm sculpture carries on. His gaze fixed into the untouchable distance, where the window-pane is as faraway as the moon.

---

five is for rich, and six is for poor. Seven for a witch, and eight for a whore. Nine for a burying, I can tell thee more.'

Chapter Two - Strength

11.46 p.m.   Friday, 16th May 2003.[40]

A time of rest and slumber. The young man, tucked under linen. His body, like a broken chair, is trapped to cast ugly shadows against the moon-lit wall.[41]

***

Jonny eases his hand upon the girl [with no name]'s waist. He can feel her side flutter as he kisses her. He knows she wants him. His thoughts drift to the girl by the stacking-system and the brightly lit girls in the kitchen. He thinks about Lisa and a billion other girls he's had, or not. Racing. His pulse. His mind. His hormones. He pulls away from the kiss and looks at the girl.

She looks back at him, wondering why he's stopped sucking out her brains. Her face is like one of those cheep blow-up dolls you see in joke shop windows.

Jonny   Come on.

He stands up and grabs her hand, as if to whisk her away to somewhere more romantic.

The girl with no name   Where we going?

She asks, with a smile – still dazed from the lack of oxygen!

---

[40] Buddha Day.
[41] It was a full moon that night.

Jonny   Somewhere.

He says, dragging her out of the room and into the busy corridor of drunken souls.

***

Everything at night seems bigger. Noises seem louder. Movements seem larger. Imaginations run riot when the light goes off.

As the young man lies sleeping his shadow flickers on the wall.

Was he moving or was it just his lungs filling with air?[42]

Was it just the movement behind his chest amplified by its projection on the wall?

But then he moved again.

This time it's his shoulder girdle twitching.[43] In response his arm jerks. And then... One of his paralysed, spay limbs twists itself straight, fanning out like the branch of a tree. From that single bone of the humerus – but it isn't funny – to the twenty-six bones of his hand, there is life!

Jonathan's eyes flicker from sleep. Pain wracks his brow as he wills the other unmovable arm to adjust from the busted bones. He strains against the prison of sheets – his heart beats as he breaks free. Escaping the warmth of the bedclothes, he is free! Emerging into the shadowed half-light of the room. Perfect. Once a Picasso, now like

---

[42] The tips of the lungs are situated behind the clavicles and the first ribs. The clavicles are two long, curving bones that rest on the sternum, just at the base of the throat. Their function is to open the arms out from the centre of the body. If we breathe, they move.

[43] The shoulder girdle rests on the ribcage, but floats free. It is attached to the skeleton only at the sternum. This allows the right arm to act independently of the left.

Michelangelo's *David*,[44] his arm is a sculpture in warm, white marble.

To touch. Slowly he raises his hand to his face – watch this space! As...

Convulsions! His body seems to celebrate as his mind struggles with a disbelief at what is happening...

He can move!

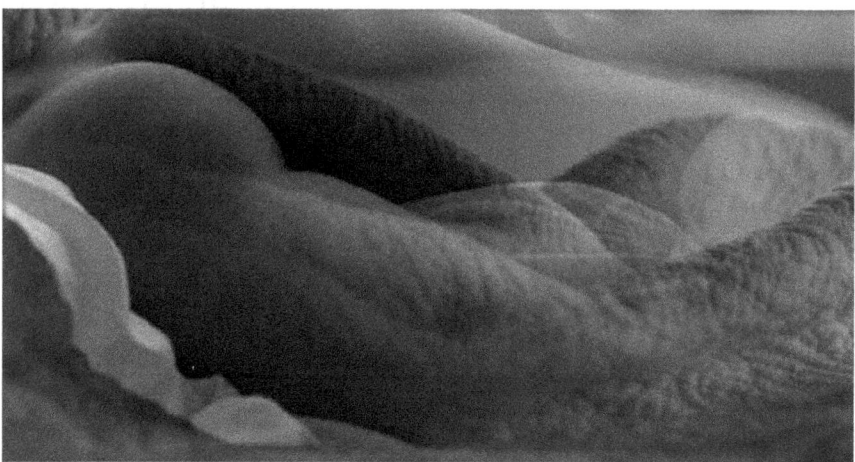

His fingers, thin, dig into the flesh of his ineffective features. They tear away at the contorted skin about his eyes and nose. The dead flesh falls onto the taut sheet, bloodless, like putty. Handfuls of wasted skin stretching and snapping from their tethers, to drop in chunks upon the bedroom floor.

The mask is removed.

---

[44] Michelangelo *(1475–1564)* is most famous for his sculpture of *David*, and his painting of the ceiling of the Sistine Chapel, in Rome. But Michelangelo was not just a sculptor, and a great painter, he was also an accomplished architect, poet and engineer. Considered by many to be one of the greatest masters of the Renaissance (a period in European history, from the 14th to the 17th century, responsible for the resurgence of classical values, expressed in the arts, literature, and the sciences). *See* Appendix IV.

Legs find form. Their once wasted disguise gone, as they straighten and smooth. He can feel his arms growing stronger, longer, no more the useless impotent limbs that once hung there, spare.

His spine – the body's moving column of support – that was twisted and fucked, straightens, like the release of a slip-knot, to drop and align.[45] The sheet, once a mountain range of twisted bones, lies flat, fluttering with the increased heartbeat of an athlete. All neat and tidy again.

Standing – the accumulated weight of the head, thorax and limbs transfers down the vertebral column to his pelvis, the bridge that spreads the weight down through his legs and into the floor.

He feels the spongy, fluid-filled discs between each of his vertebrae self-adjust[46] as he moves.[47] He feels the sensation of the floor supporting him through the centre of his feet, up through his thigh sockets and back, to the base of his head. He feels his bones living and changing.[48] The weight of his body passing back down through his spine, spreading out through his pelvis, and down through his legs and feet into the floor.

---

[45] Alignment of the spine affects the entire functioning of the body. It is said that the spine is two inches shorter on earth than it is in space. The downward pull of gravity compressing the discs. (*See* Appendix V)

[46] It takes twenty minutes for these discs to re-inflate after lying flat on your back for any great length of time.

[47] These discs protect the spinal nerves as they emerge from the cord and make up a quarter of the total length of the spine, being proportionally larger in the more flexible areas of the spine.

[48] It's the bones that make the body's red blood cells.

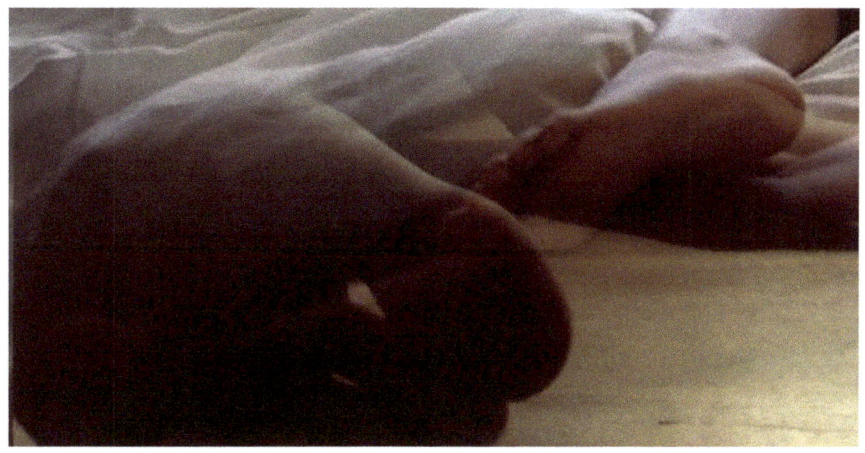

Then... Again... Shaky, like a foal taking its first clumsy steps away from its mother... After almost seven years of lifelessness.

Alone he stands in front of the wardrobe mirror[49] and he looks at his reflection for the first time since his accident. Nervously he peels off the hideous pyjamas that they only dress cripples in. He lets the clothing fall to the carpet.[50]

Naked. He looks at his reflection. His body has changed so much in the years that have passed. He sees a man gazing back at him. A hymn with different words, but the same unmistakable tune. He'd have recognised it anywhere. Standing there. Staring back at himself. Rearranged.

He looks at the catheter,[51] fitted into his side. The warm brown bag taped 'discretely' – excretely – to his thigh. Slowly he pulls the tube from his body – it gives a sigh, as it leaves. The wound is dry. No pain. Just relief. He is free of it all now.

---

[49] A thing he has avoided since the accident.
[50] The skeleton renews itself over twenty times during the course of our lives.
[51] A tube fitted into the body to remove urine and excrement.

>...And there composed
> > formed in sinew and skin
> > the moving orchestration of cells
> > played out in form and substance
> > the visual music of muscular notes
> > picked out beneath his skin's soft melody
> > and accompanied by the beat of his heart
> > > the laboured rhythm of his breath
> > > and all the thoughts that rush through his mind
> > > > like sand through time
> > > > he is his own cacophony
> > > > > 'till peace is restored
> > > > > and rest

But how? Now is not the time for questions. He just wants to look. To touch. Handle the goods...

Twenty-two. Very nearly twenty-three. But he – not been he for so long – thought all the time about one thing. Would he walk? Would he talk? The one last part of him that still slept... And with one touch Sleeping Beauty[52] arose... 'by any other name...' lifted his weary head slowly from his slumber, and stood.

Massaging life into the limp body of his cock, he crows to himself that he had returned – like Lazarus[53] – from the grave...

***

Jonny and the girl [with no name] were alone at last, in the privacy of Julie's parents' bedroom. A pink paradise of pretty floral designs and chintz. And as the door was closed behind them, they began.

It was dark,[54] but that didn't matter because their eyes were shut tight.

---

[52] Who was put to sleep for a hundred years by a 'prick' on her finger!
[53] Lazarus was the man Jesus brought back from the dead. *(New Testament: Luke 16:19-31)*
[54] They didn't switch on the light.

It was as though someone had started a stop-watch as they locked into a kiss and fell back onto the bed. Racing one another, they removed their clothes, in a frantic pulling and tugging. Eyes still closed. Mouths still soldered together. They were like two escapologists wriggling out of straight-jackets, suspended by their lips from a smouldering body. *Free!*

In their underwear they could feel their skin against skin.

Jonny's hand grabbed at one of the girl's breasts. She winced in pain. But he wouldn't be there for long. His rough touch wasn't pleasant, but it was passionate. She knew this and let it go without a sound. In a moment his hand was in her knickers. His cock sticking out from the fly of his sticky boxers. His finger sliding into the moist little slit of her cunt. He could feel it squelch as he flicked his middle-finger in and out of her. She moaned and he moaned. And soon they were both naked and the kiss was broken. Eyes wide open.

Jonny searched for his jeans… His wallet… And the condom he'd brought with him.

Triumphant!

He showed her the foil square. No words were spoken as he prepared himself. She just lay back and got herself comfy.

He positioned himself between her legs as she tilted her pelvis for him. He dropped himself onto his hands and they kissed. Then – supporting himself on his left hand – he started to brutishly guide his dick into her tight little hole with his right hand. Banging it into her bone a couple of times until he'd found his way in. The kissing stopped as he concentrated on the task at hand. He nuzzled into her neck as she clung to his back.

Thrusting as deep as he could – with all his might… Girls like that![55]

---

[55] He imagined.

Once – Twice – Three times…
Four – Five…
6…
7… 8…
8 ½… *(just a minute)*…

… **Aaaaarr**rrgg*ghhh*!

…and it was over...

STOP THE CLOCK!

00hrs.02min.39sec.15

From the door closing to ejaculation. Jonny now knew that if the UK was to be hit with a nuclear warhead, he would be capable of having sex with blonde twins, with huge tits, before he died.

He pulled himself out, flopped onto his back and wrenched off the Durex. He lay motionless. His heart pounding. His arse sweating. His dick flopping. And his eyes drooping…

'It doesn't get much better than this' he thought to himself and smiled.

The girl with no name turned and snuggled into him – it was as though she'd just asked him to meet her parents. Jonny was up and out of the bed faster than a dog shitting in his master's slippers.

The girl with no name   What's the matter?

Jonny was already half dressed.

Jonny   Nothin'. I'll meet you downstairs.

And with that he was gone…

The girl with no name hauled herself off the bed and into her clothes.

***

…Michelangelo's *David* stood there with a Jackson Pollock[56] dribbling down the wardrobe mirror…

---

[56] Jackson Pollock *(1912–56)* was an Action Painter who dripped and smeared paint on his canvases to express rather than illustrate.

Chapter Three - Gateway

9.12 a.m.   Saturday, 17th May 2003.

Jonathan sits in his chair gazing out of the window.

In a lifetime the human eye will take in over 24 million different images. Jonathan will take in less than a third... Unless his mother varies his diet, or cuts down the tree in the back garden, neither of which is likely.

The human body needs something to stimulate it, or it will create its own stimulation.[57]

Not seeing people is difficult... Seeing the same faces day-in-day-out is not much better.[58]

Boredom becomes your greatest enemy. You lose your mind. You climb the walls.[59] You feel the room closing in on you and crushing your skull in a vice-like grip...

---

[57] David Blaine *(born in Brooklyn, 4th April, 1973)* is best known for his street magic and his Endurance Art. In *Above the Below* Blaine suspended himself 100 ft above the River Thames (London) in a Plexiglas box, seven feet deep, seven feet long and three feet wide. He had no food and no contact with the outside world for 44 days. The event began on Friday, 5th September, 2003, at 8.30 p.m. (and ended at 9.00 p.m. on Sunday, 19th October). He talked about how the body learns to adapt to its circumstances, and how his levels of appreciation for the simple things – such as a smile or a sunset – become more intense. His reason for doing this? To attempt to live his life 'beautifully'... His other events have included: *Alive* (5th April, 1999) – when he was buried under six feet of water for 7 days – *Frozen In Time* (27th November, 2000) – when he was encased in six tones of ice for 3 days in Time Square – *Vertigo* (21st May, 2002) – when he stood on a pillar, 100 ft above 42nd Street (New York) for a day and a half. (*See* Further Crippled)
[58] A rut is just a shallow grave.

Basically, you go mad in stages...

Jonathan had escaped it, so far... He lived in his head. That was his reality. The physical world was merely a virtual space where his body was held in a state of suspended animation...

Or that's how it feels...

In his mind he's capable of journeying to other places. Of seeing and experiencing things, just like we all do in our physical world. And each day, in his mind, he writes his journal of the things he's done and the places he's been... Don't worry, he's not mad. He knows these are dreams. He knows he's a cripple!

My dreams became more and more vivid. Last night it was as though I had broken free of my body. For the first time in almost eight years I could walk again.

This time, however, it was different. Usually his dreams were in *Cinemascope*. He watched himself like a character in a glorious *Technicolor* movie - complete with scintillating dialogue and sparkling studio sets, things were immaculate, all *Gone with the Wind* and Rogers and Hammerstein.[60] But this time it was different. This time he wasn't 'watching' himself, this time he *was* himself, as though he were the camera, viewing the action through his own eyes.[61] And the senses, they felt so real. As though...[62]

But it was just a dream. It wasn't anything more than a vivid dream.[63]

He knew that way madness lies![64]

---

[59] Metaphorically, of course!
[60] Rogers and Hammerstein were the writers of 1950s movie musicals like *The Sound of Music*, *The King and I* and *South Pacific*.
[61] In 'first person' rather than in 'third person' as an invisible voyeur.
[62] *See* Appendix V.
[63] *See* Appendix VI.

***

David was stood outside HMV[65] having a fag, waiting for Charlie...

Charlie Wanna get a coffee?

Charlie was a girl, an Art student, dark hair and eyes.

David OK!

They walked to the coffee shop on the corner – ordered two cappuccinos – and got themselves a table.

David So? How was it?

Charlie *(with a giggle in her voice)* Fuck you!

David smiled and swept back the fringe from his eyes.

David Come on… You know you want to tell me.

CharlieI *so* do not.

David *(now it was his turn to have a giggle in his voice)* That bad?

---

[64] From the quote in Shakespeare's *King Lear* (Act III, Scene 4) 'O! that way madness lies; let me shun that.'

[65] H.M.V– the initials stand for His Master's Voice – the original name of the company that once produced records (the precursor to Compact Discs) and record-players. The company logo was a small dog, called Nipper, listening to a record playing on a gramophone (another word for 'record-player').

And the conversation was as frothy as the coffee, and as light and bright as the day…

Charlie   Fuck off!

David   You *so* want him.

Charlie   I do not.

David   So what's the big deal then?

Charlie   There is no *'big deal'*.

David   So tell me then.

Charlie   No!

David   You *so* want him.

Charlie   Fuck off! Stop saying that.

David   Then tell me. What's he like?

Charlie   *(in a girl scream of shocked delight)* No!

David   Come on. I'll buy you a muffin.

Charlie   No.

David   Charlie?

Charlie   OK…

She'd done enough protesting for her to believe she'd been forced into *'spilling the beans'*…

    …We met in the Union bar…

David   …Very romantic.

Charlie   Do you want to hear, or not?

David coyly mimed locking his lips and Charlie began again.

Charlie   We met in the Union and went on to Canal Street.

David   *(with explosive glee)* I knew it! He's a puff![66]

Charlie   No he isn't! We went to Prague V, Berlin's…

David   …Classy…

He was being sarcastic. Berlin's left a lot to be desired

Charlie   …and then back to his.

***

His mother – regular as prunes – came into his room with a bowl of hot water ready for his wash.

Mother   Are you ready for your wash now?

And in his mind, he talks.

Mum?

Mother   First your handies…

She gives his floppy hands a quick tickle with the face cloth. Let's face it, how the fuck is a quadriplegic going to get his hands dirty?

Mum! Last night I walked…

But no one hears.

---

[66] Canal Street is the gay-quarter of Manchester hosting sixteen bars and three clubs.

Mother   …Then our chinny-win-win…

She bed-baths his face, sanding down three layers of skin to a clinically clean layer somewhere beyond red-raw.

I know it was just a dream, but it felt so real.

Mother   There! That wasn't too bad was it?

No, not when you've got no sensation of pain in your body.

Mother   And now we're all clean again.

I wish you could hear me.

But she gave up trying a long time ago. Just like all the rest.

And then she leaves.

And then it's silent once again.

Maybe I'm going mad?

***

Hours pass. Feels like days. Hazy lazy days. Of months, and years, and *'seasons in the sun…'*

And beyond the window he can see life.

A young man, about Jonathan's age, is waiting at the bus stop.

Who are you? I see you there almost every day. You catch the Number forty-two into town. I wonder where you go when you get there. I wonder what you do. I call you David.[67] I've invented a whole life for you in my head. But you don't know that.

---

[67] David, a Hebrew name meaning 'beloved'.

I've worked out that you are an Art student. You carry one of those plastic fishing boxes. The sort of thing Art students put their stuff in. Sometimes you have one of those big black folders. So you must be an Art student – or a fisherman with a very large wallet. You usually wear a dark combat jacket, ripped, faded jeans, and trainers by Nike. Your hair is white-blonde – long with a floppy fringe. You smoke! I don't know what brand. I guess it's something cheap if you're a student. You probably study at the University. I guess you're about my age... And that's about as much as I know, for sure. But what I make up is something quite different...

***

Right, readers, let's get this straight from the start. I'm not a retard – I'm a quadriplegic. It's not contagious. I'm not deaf – so you don't have to shout when you talk to me... And I'm not simple. It's just that I don't look too good in a swim-suit, that's all... Apart from that I'm quite normal... Whatever that is... I just had an accident... Fucked my body up a bit... It's just the outside...People have problems coping with the outside...

***

Jonny's job was done, and he could enjoy the rest of the party, with the knowledge that his evening's mission had been completed...

So, there he was in the living-room.

Could he help it if the attractive girl sat by the stacking-system wanted to chat?

Could he help it if she wanted a little company on this hot summer night?

Could he help it if she just happened to kiss him?

Could he help it if somebody else just happened to walk in at that moment?

Point of fact: *At no point during the evening did Jonny express a desire to be faithful, or exclusive, with any person, or persons, mentioned in the above document. Nor was any contract, verbal or otherwise, entered into with any said person, or persons, mentioned in the above document. Ergo, he was single and therefore quite within his rights to 'get off' with who the fuck he wanted to 'get off' with. So there!*

The *'someone else'* just happened to be the girl with no name. She wasn't impressed. She took one look at Jonny, with his tonsils wrapped around Little Miss Stacking-System, with such veracity... If looks could kill, she would have levelled most of Western Europe. And then she ran out of the room to escape it all...

Jonny felt guilty... Even though *'technically'* he wasn't doing anything wrong, and felt it only right he should follow her and explain... He was a gentleman, after all.

Jonny   *(to Little Miss Stacking-System)* I won't be a minute...

Well he wasn't going to give up this one – he hadn't had her yet!

Anyway, he followed the girl with no name out into the front garden.

The poor girl was distraught.

Jonny   What's the matter?

He knew, but felt that ignorance may be the best form of defence.

The girl with no name   What do you mean, what's the matter? You were getting off with that girl.

Jonny   *(using the same tactics as before)* So?

The girl with no name   I thought...

Halfway through the sentence she realises how stupid she was going to appear – having made an assumption, based on an incident lasting less than three minutes.

…You know…

Jonny   Sorry.

Now this was a great move. Was he sorry for kissing someone else? Was he sorry for hurting her feelings? Or was he just sorry he shagged her? She had to work that one out for herself – because, as far as he was concerned, he was guilt-free and in the clear – and on his way back to Little Miss Stacking-System…

Chapter Four - Signals

12.27 p.m. Saturday, 17th May 2003.

Jonathan's bedroom.

He's a million miles away – in his mind. His mother comes in with his lunch.

Mother   Are you ready for your lunch?

She drapes a tea towel around his neck, like a baby's bib.

It was sausage and mash before it was fed into the blender. Now it resembled the contents of his colostomy bag.[68]

Mother   Open wide like a good boy.

Everyday he tries to talk to her in his head.

> Come on, open your mouth for Mummy.

And in *her* head she talks to him...

Come on, you bloody cripple, eat!

Sometimes it gets too much. She gets as frustrated with herself as she does with him. But on the outside, it can never show.

---

[68] A colostomy bag holds the waste produced by the colon and acts as an anus for those who cannot evacuate their faecal waste for themselves. The waste produced by the body goes into the bag via a catheter.

Mother   Isn't that nice? Yum-yum-yum!

And on the inside…

You hate me, don't you?

But this was her son…

Mother   Want some more?

I can tell by your eyes.

Mother   Is this Jonathan's favourite dinner? I think it is.

She talks to him like a baby because there is no other way of knowing him. And she remembers how proud she was of him, and how quick he was to walk. How quick he was to talk... And all that's gone now.

It's as though he's moved out and left *this* behind – like washing that she does out of duty... Begrudgingly...

You resent me, don't you?

His appetite is lost. All is lost…

Mother   What's the matter? Had enough?

Thank Christ for that!

I'm sorry, Mum.

Mother   Are you all full up now?

You'll never know how thankful I am for all you've done for me.

Mother   Let's just give your face a wipe.

You mucky bugger.

She uses the bib to scrape off the food from around his mouth.

Mother   There! Isn't that better? And while we're at it, we'll change your bag…

She hates this.

Pissy, shitty, horrible thing… I hate this, I really hate this.

As she unfastens the tube from the bag, the stench of warm shit fills the room. It's a rancid, festering smell. It a smell that never goes away. It holds itself in your nose and on your clothes. It becomes your hands and your hair. You never feel clean – no matter how much bleach or disinfectant you use – the smell is always there.[69] Like a memory.

I know what you think, as you're changing my bag. And it's degrading to me too.

He twitches involuntary. She doesn't want shit all over the carpet – again!

Oh, keep still, for Christ's sake!

Her words are meant to soothe him.

Mother   Temper! Temper! Mummy's going as fast as she can. I know it's not very nice, but it won't take a minute.

A change of subject, for the benefit of both of them.

---

[69] To remove urine stains from washable fabrics you first need to soak the article you wish to clean in cold water, for 3–4 hours, in an enzyme-based washing powder. Follow the washing instructions on the item being cleaned and wash as directed (adding a product such as Shout to your washing). Treat old stains with a hydrogen peroxide solution (first twist the fabric around the stain to prevent the solution from spreading to the rest of fabric) and apply it only to the stain, then rinse thoroughly. Always remember to use bleach carefully.

Mother   Your auntie Enid's coming over this afternoon. Are you going to sit in the garden with us?

Do I have a choice?

Look at the time. I better get my skates on.

Mother   Just time to tidy up before she gets here. Now, you be a good boy for Mummy while I do my jobs, and I'll bring you a nice drink of juice when I've finished.

You mean when you remember.

And then she goes.

***

The party was over. Jonny was pissed. He'd had his shag. He'd *'got off'* with all the eligible skirt within a five-mile radius of the building. And had his middle-finger in at least three of them, from what he could remember. As for his own *'tackle'* – he'd been groped by at least a dozen. Eight or nine of those had actually had their hands in his boxers. And two had given him a blow-job. So he couldn't complain. He'd had a good night. And now it was time to go home.

It was half-two in the morning. The buses had stopped running and Jonny decided the best course of action would be to flag down a taxi. He headed for the main road. He was drunk. The world swirled about him. He couldn't focus. His eyes half shut. He was falling and stumbling at every step. It was a battle just to keep upright, never mind walk… But he managed to get himself to the main road.

He saw a car. There was a 50/50 chance of it being a taxi. He stepped out to flag it down. He misjudged the distance. He stumbled. He lurched. He was in the path of the car. Too close. No time for the driver to… Didn't see him – too late… He tried to swerve. He couldn't…

Skreeeech... Thud... Crunch...!

The car hit him at 40 mph, shattering his legs. It picked him up like a matador[70] and threw him on the bonnet, crashing him into the windscreen. All blood and broken glass. He hit the pavement like a paper bag full of tomato soup. His last movements were balletic. A poetic aesthetic of cradling steel and expressive limbs. Twisted and distorted. His skull – fucked.[71] His body paralysed. This is how Michelangelo became Picasso. This is how Jonny became Jonathan.

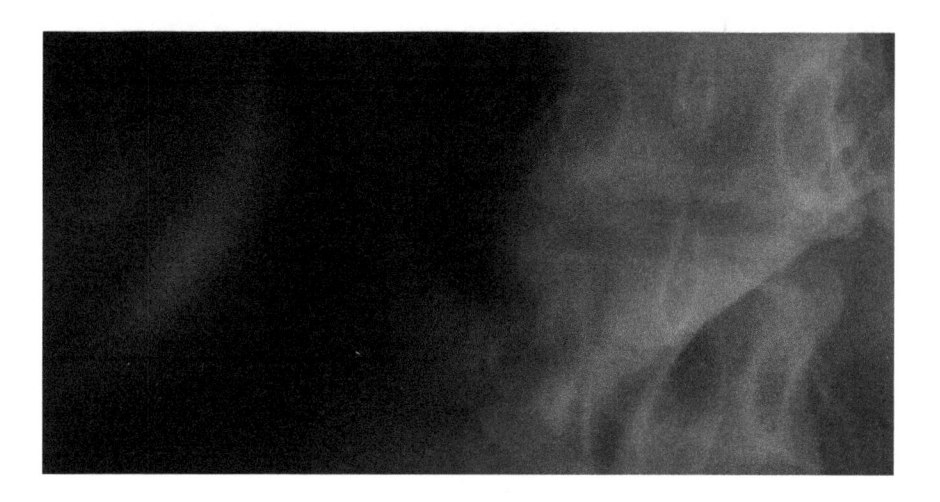

***

The accident had damaged his spinal cord. The force of the impact fucking his spine, resulting in vertebral fractures and subluxations, causing expressive aphasia[72] due to the dammed middle cerebral artery[73].

---

[70] A matador is the principal bullfighter who, during a bull fight, is responsible for finally killing the bull.
[71] The head is made up of twenty-nine bones. Eight bones form the cranium. Fourteen bones form the face. Half of these had been broken as they hit the windscreen.
[72] He couldn't speak!
[73] The speech centres.

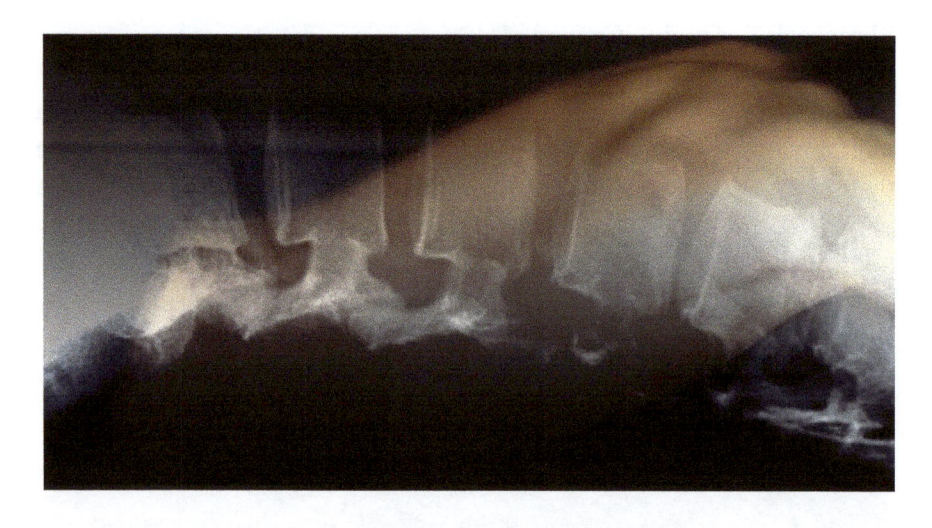

Inside the protection of the skull floats the brain. Its nerve endings flow down the spinal cord and separate into the sciatic nerves at the sacrum, and then continue on down to the tips of the toes. The clear cerebro-spinal fluid, produced in the centre of the brain, bathes the spinal cord. It pulses down to the base of the spine and then returns, [74] in a constant tide of connection between head and pelvis.

All this was fucked up now…

>   The relationship between the sides.
>   would never be the same again.
>   the sum of too many angles
>   twisted, bent out of shape
>   deformed dreams
>   of what could have been
>   The wasted time spent
>   worrying and nagging
>   of nights taken up with Pythagoras
>   a theorem for nothing...
>   when all the side add up to zero.

***

---

[74] 9 to 10 times per minute.

David felt the sun shining in through the window, warm on his face. As he lay in bed, he contemplated his day, and opened his eyes.

His room was a student abode of tired wallpaper and carpet you don't want to walk on in bare feet. It always felt damp. Posters covered up the bad bits. He had lots of posters. Including the iconic Che[75] and obligatory Escher[76] prints. And this was his.

His home away from home. A student flat in a manky old Victorian house, all tall walls and high peeling ceilings. A bastard to heat from the single bar electric fire. So you don't bother. Too expensive anyhow. But today was bright, and sunny, and his room was lit with warmth that made his eyes smile. And not just because it was free.

---

[75] Che Guevara *(1928–1967)* – Ernesto *'Che'* Guevara was an Argentine-born hero of the Latin American Communist revolution in Cuba. A confidant of Cuba's leader, Fidel Castro, his Christ-like image has adorned student T-shirts, pin-badges and posters since the 1960s – becoming as iconic as Marilyn Monroe and James Dean.

[76] M. C. Escher *(1898–1972)* - Maurits Cornelis Escher is probably one of the most popular graphic artists of the 20th century. His work is reproduced in many forms and is typified by his use of clever effects that 'trick' the eye and defy the laws of physics. (*See* **Further Crippled**)

Chapter Five - Journey

2.48 p.m.   Saturday, 17th May 2003.

In the back, garden Jonathan sat in his chair. His mother and her friend Enid were there too, hitting the gin. Mother had started earlier to get herself in the mood before Enid arrived. It wasn't unusual for them to get through a litre of Gordon's in an afternoon, while he sat there watching them get slowly pissed, listening to the in's and out's and round-a-bout's of church gossip. Both Carol and Enid worshipped at the Church of St Michael's – the patron saint of middle-class women.[77]

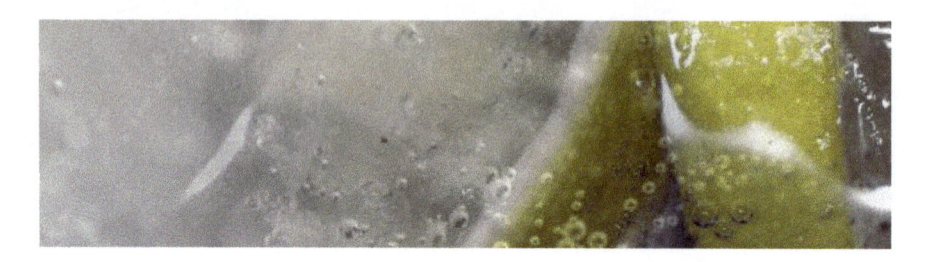

This was when his mother[78] came alive.

Carol   …Well I'm telling you. That young vicar said to me, "Carol," he said, "if we were meant to live without sin, God wouldn't have given us churches, would he?" Well, I looked at him, and he looked at Mrs. Kaplan. I knew what he was after saying. Well, she's been knocking-off that plumber from number 15, hasn't she?

---

[77] St Michael has been the brand name of Marks & Spencer's good since 1927.
[78] Carol.

Enid looked surprised.

Carol   Didn't you know? I thought it was common knowledge. Ooo, let me fill you in on the details...

And that's what it's like for four hours. A blow by blow account of who's fucking who, and who's said what and why... It's the most un-Christian thing you've ever heard.

But for them it passed the day...

Carol   Oh, Jonathan and I are fine. Aren't we, love?

She says. Giving a cursory nod in Jonathan's general direction.

Enid   I worry about you, you know. Well, it can't be easy for you, can it?

Every time she speaks, her head wobbles like an oscillating electric fan set on medium blow.

Carol   We get by. I find him a comfort, sometimes. You know, now Bob's dead.

Enid   You've the patience of a saint.

Patience is just despair disguised as a virtue.

Enid   There's not many that'd do what you you've done. Most would have had him put in a Home.

That word - 'Home' - it should fill you with a sense of security. Images of a warm fire and loving family... But when you're helpless... When your body's fucked up and you don't know shit from sugar, the meaning is something quite different. The word changes...

She changes the subject.

Carol   Another drink?

Enid   Just a little one.

A glass is poured.

Enid   I heard that new school teacher's been having it off with *thingy* from the butchers.

In their world, everyone loved a gossip.

Carol   Never!

Enid   True as I'm sat here.

Not that she was one to judge.

Carol   But he's married with children.

Enid   Two. One boy. One girl.

Her voice grated like a fucked up first-generation thermal fax machine that needed its band tightening.

Carol   Does his wife know?

Enid   What do you think?

Gin sloshed out of her glass as she repositioned herself in the garden chair.

Carol   How long's he been seeing her then?

Enid   Your guess is as good as mine. But it must be a couple of months at least.

Carol hung on every word.

Carol   Why do you say that?

Enid   Because Gladys, who does the altar flowers, swears she's pregnant - but you didn't hear that from me, and you haven't to tell anyone… If it gets out, she could lose her job.

Carol   What? The teacher?

This was scandal of the highest order.

Enid   No. Gladys. Apparently, she was told it in trust. She has the vicar's ear you know. Oh, yes. Nothing happens in the Parish without Gladys knowing…

And so it goes on and Jonathan thinks of the boy at the bus stop.

***

Rusholme is home to Manchester's Curry Mile[79] and hosts a number of affordable student houses. Tom lived in one of these desirable residences over a curry shop. The neon-sign above the shop giving his room a character unique to this part of town. It was like *Blade Runner*, the Cheap Cut. But it was okay, and handy for a take-away.

---

[79] With 62 restaurants in the one mile.

Charlie   Nice.

That covered it.

But they hadn't come to talk. They'd come to fuck! Not shag. Not bang. But to fuck. And with the Soho neon, and air filled with cumin, it was ideal.

Tom was tall and dark. She was dark and feminine. In vodka-fuelled ecstasy they imagined themselves in a Hindu temple, fusing their bodies in the sacred rites of Shiva.[80] In reality they were rolling around on the carpet of a stinky little bedsit in the arse-end of Manchester. But let's not spoil the moment…

In his arms she felt safe and warm. His smooth body complimented hers, as they kissed and stroked one another. The roughness of his chin against her neck. The smell of his aftershave. The masculine touch of his hands. She felt lifted out of herself. As though she was dancing in the clouds above the city. He was gentle, and kind, and tender, and she wanted to love him. She wanted to know him from his childhood to his grave. And when he entered her. And when he entered her… She could feel him fuse with her. Feel him… Feel him… The rhythm of his body etching onto hers the meaning of what it felt like to be in *exstasis*.[81]

> feeling like E to the F'd
> clenched jaw to stop the spirit leaving
> and it flies around the blood with a buzz
> of Manchester bees and twisted mellow…
>   All the dark clubs sweats –
> At one with the god
>   and he dances in,
>   and through,
>   and on…

---

[80] Hindu god of creation and destruction.
[81] *See* Appendix VIII.

***

David   And then what?

Charlie had fallen silent.

Charlie   You know.

David   So you shagged him then?

Charlie   Of course not.

Even with the shocked inflection it didn't sound convincing.

Charlie   OK… We shagged. Happy now?

David   Seeing him again?

Charlie   Don't know.

But she wished she did. She wanted to.

***

The afternoon had passed and Enid had gone. Jonathan was pushed back inside and up to his room. To be put away like the best china, until the visitors came round again and he could be wheeled out and displayed once more. He was the symbol of her humanity, her martyrdom, her compassion. Without him she had no purpose, no focus, no function.

Chapter Six - Opening

11-36 a.m.   Monday, 19th May 2003.

The bus stop.

David had a Life Class[82] that morning. He was late. He'd probably skip it. By the time he got there it would be over anyway. He'd just go into town and see what was happening. He was missing a lot of classes lately. The nights were getting to him. For some reason he couldn't sleep, and when he did, he woke up tired.

He noticed someone watching him and glanced them a look.

Jon   Hi!

David   Hi.

At least it wasn't a freak! You get a lot of freaks at bus stops.

Jon   You're one of the Art students, aren't you?

---

[82] Life Classes are where art students create work from 'life' (nude) models.

David   Ye'.

Jon   I've seen you around.

David didn't know how to take this. He couldn't say the same thing back. And a silence followed as the conversation ended. He looked for a bus to save him.

Jon   Should be one here in a minute. They're supposed to run every fifteen minutes.

David   You at the Uni then?

How was he supposed to answer this?

Jon   Ye'. Medicine. Anatomy.

At least he could bluff his way through that one.

David   You know a lad called Jason? From Newcastle.

Jon   Don't think so. I don't know that many people on my course.

David   You'll know my friend – Charlie?

And the bus arrived! And Jonathan thanked god.

Jon   *(he'd had thinking time)* Ye', we have some friends in common.

They talked as the bus shunted them through the Eastern hamlets of suburban Manchester.

David   I didn't get your name?

Jon   Jon, short for Jonathan.

David   David, short for David. So, where'd you go out to? I must admit I haven't seen you around or anything.

You wouldn't would you. I never leave my room.

Jon   Ye'. I don't tend to go out very much.

David   But its Manchester. Everyone goes out in Manchester.

Unless you're a quadriplegic living at home with your mother!

Jon   Not me. I guess I'm just boring.

I sound such a geek!

David   You'll have to come out with me and Charlie sometime.

Jon   Sure!

David   This is my stop. I'll see you around.

Jon   See you around.

And he was gone.

What's happening?

***

Hospitals have a smell all of their own.

And as Jonathan's mother and father waited for the doctor. They held onto the hope that everything would be all right. They came from a generation that believed in miracles, from a time that had seen great medical breakthroughs: Heart transplants, and brain surgery, and replacement fucking hips.

And then the doctor arrived…

Doctor   We did everything we could…

Carol's heart stopped. This is how they tell you your only son's dead.

Doctor   But the injuries to his spinal cord were very severe… He has total paralysis. I'm sorry…

Mother   But he will get better, won't he?

He's not dead!

Doctor   I'm sorry…

And she wailed like a Banshee. Her husband, his father, could barely support her. Her paralysis began that night too.

Father   What happens now?

Doctor   It really is too early to say. But in cases such as your son's, where there is a likelihood of severe brain damage… Now I know it's hard to think about things like this right now, but you need to be aware of some of the long-term implications of this.

But they drifted in and out of the words. Nothing much made sense.

Doctor   …It's important to think about the quality of life… Not just for him, but for you too. A patient with this level of paralysis demands an extremely high level of care, and with the best will in the world…

And all she could say in response was.

Mother   He's not going into a Home!

Father   Carol…

Mother   No! He's our son. I want to take him home.

Doctor   He's going to need round-the-clock specialist care. He won't be able to walk, feed himself, even go to the bathroom on his own. Chances are he won't even know who you are, or where he is. You don't have to make any decisions now. But there are other options I think you both should consider, for his benefit as well as yours.

MotherHe's my son. And that's all that matters.

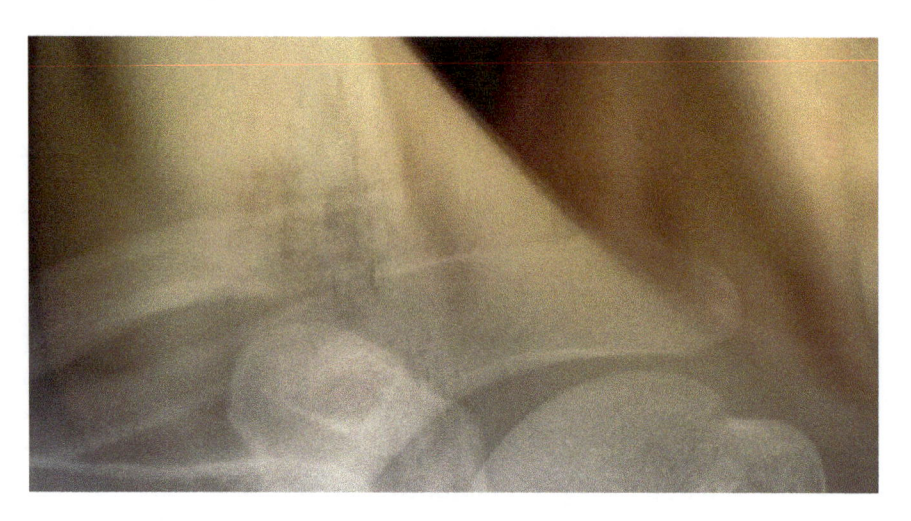

And with that, Jonathan came home.

***

Nero's, Manchester.

David   I met a friend of yours today.

Charlie   Who?

David   Jon? Does Medicine?

She searches her memory for the name.

Charlie   The name doesn't ring any bells?

David   You have some friends in common or something?

Charlie   Can't put a face to him.

David   Seems OK

Charlie   Did you go to class, in the end?

And then he was forgotten.

Chapter Seven - Gift

X

3.36 p.m.   Tuesday, 20th May 2003.

Carol's back garden. To set the scene would be pointless. It was like Groundhog Day.[83] Same patio, same panel fence, same patchy grass trying to grow through the same resilient bindweed.[84]

And there, amongst it all, are the two gin-soaked ladies of a certain age, sat beside a cripple in a wheelchair.

This is the stuff that hell is made of. They drink to forget. Forgetting is another form of freedom.

Carol   That young lad's back.

She had seen David getting off the bus stop.

        He's one of those students.

---

[83] The phrase 'Groundhog Day' comes from the title of a 1993 movie, and refers to a situation that is continually repeating itself, as if in a loop, infinitum.
[84] Bindweed – *Calystegia sepium* – commonly known as Hedge bindweed, a lawn weed that effects uncultivated ground, paths, drives and lawns.

Enid (*craning her neck*) I've never seen him before. Mind you, if I was a couple of years younger.

They cackle. Enid's laugh sounded like that noise dogs make, just before they're about to throw up.

Carol Oh, Enid, give over!

Edith (*calling loudly over the fence*) Coo-ee!

Leave him alone, you drunken bitch.

Carol Give over. You'll have the neighbours looking.

Enid I don't care. We're both single women.

Enid lifted her head back and stretched out her neck.[85] This was her finest Bette Davis[86] pose, and the one she'd seen Joan Collins[87] performing in most of her episodes in *Dynasty*[88].

Carol And old enough to know better.

She giggled.

Enid Look, he's gone all shy.

So had Carol.

Carol I'm not surprised. You're embarrassing the poor lad.

---

[85] This tightens the neck's skin and removes the appearance of wrinkles.
[86] Bette Davis (1908–1989) – one of the Hollywood's greatest actresses. She made over 100 films in a career than spanned over sixty years. She was nominated for Academy Awards ten times, and won twice.
[87] Joan Collins (b.1933) – an actress most famous for her role as Alexis Carrington in the 1980s US soap opera *Dynasty*. She was married five times and seen by many as synonymous with her on screen role of Alexis.
[88] *Dynasty* – an American primetime soap opera about wealthy oil barons. The show ran from 1981–89.

Oh, please leave him alone.

Enid   I don't think so.

David walked off up the road. Head down. Eyes down.

Enid   Anyway, it's been nice seeing you. I'll pop round later on next week. Catch up on the latest gossip. *(then her tone changed)* See you, Jonathan. Look after your mum, won't you![89] She needs looking after, *(she cackles)* especially with the new bus stop boy waiting outside her bedroom window.

Carol   Give over!

Enid   Give over, yourself! I saw the way you were looking at him. You can't hide things from me, Carol Simms. I've known you far too long for that.

She'd been caught out.

Carol   Go on you, before I say something.

Enid   Your secret's safe with me. I won't tell a soul.

And with that she is out of the garden gate and heading towards home.

Carol   *(shouting after her)* Bye!

Enid   *(shouting back)* Just remember, be careful with him!

Carol   Go on! *(to Jonathan)* Ooo, your auntie Enid is funny.

And then she's back her real, little world, with the gate closed firmly on the outside and all that I might bring.

---

[89] Patronising cow!

Mother   Now, love, what would you like for your tea? How about a nice sausage casserole and green beans?

I think that's what it said on the can.

Mother   Sound nice?

Wait 'till you see it.

Mother   And then we'll have some nice chocky pudding to finish with. What do you say?

I don't know why I bother. The lad's never going to answer.

I wonder what he's doing now... The lad at the bus stop was very good looking, and they do say younger men go for older women – 'experience' they call it.

And then she catches herself in her day-dream.

Mother   Ooo! I was miles away then. Silly Mummy, day-dreaming again. I'll go and put the tea on.

***

Carol started hitting the bottle when her husband died. Not that she had a problem with it. It just kept her on an even keel. He didn't die spectacularly, with a car-crash or anything. He just got up one morning, complained about chest pains and was dead by lunch-time. That was him all over really. Pretty unspectacular.

***

David got in and made himself a cup of tea. He flicked on the TV. His choice was two channels of kids' programmes, some bollocks on BBC2 or *Countdown* on Channel Four. He texts Charlie.

               Wot u up 2?

Charlie: Nothin'!

               Fancy goin out 2nite?

Charlie: OK!

               Meet U after LGB.[90] XXX

---

[90] LGB – the initials, and acronym, of the Lesbian, Gay & Bisexual Society at Manchester University.

Chapter Eight - Joy

8.43 p.m.   Tuesday, 20th May 2003.

David was waiting for a bus into town. His day had bored him. He hoped the night would be better. He felt like everyone else was moving around him – but he was somehow stuck. He needed something to unstick him. He needed a jolt to release him – and he was praying Charlie and cheap drinks would do it.

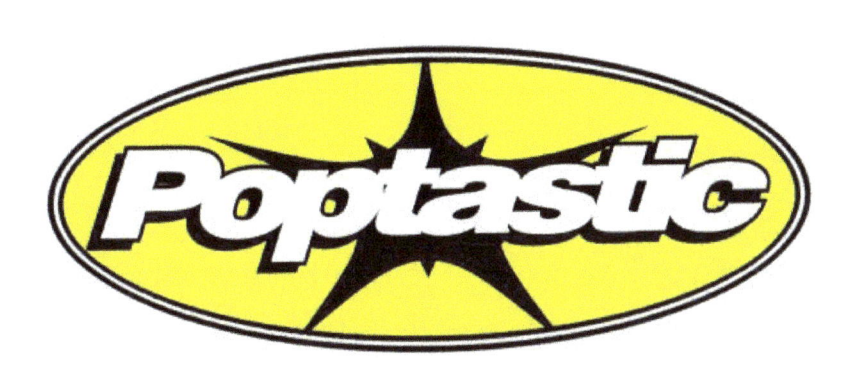

***

Tuesday night. 11.30 p.m. *Poptastic*. A subterranean club, off Princess Street, in the heart of Manchester. £5 entrance into two rooms of music.[91] All drinks £1.10. And so busy you'd think it was the weekend. It's wall-to-wall 18–30s. Someone for everyone. All pissed. All dancing. All 'mad for it'. And then…

David   *(shouting over the music)* I need to get bolloxed!

Charlie   *(shouting back)* I need a slash!

---
[91] Camp trash and alternative.

And with that she disappeared to join the queue wading in the ladies. David pushed himself through the throbbing masses at the bar and bought a Reef.[92] He turned around and saw Jon.

Jon   *(shouting over the music)* I thought I saw you!

David   *(shouting back)* What?

Jon   *(shouting over the music)* I thought I saw you!

David   *(shouting)* Jon! From the bus stop…

Jon   *(shouting)* Ye'!

David   *(shouting)* Charlie's here! She just went for a piss! I thought you didn't go out?

Jon   *(shouting)* I don't! This is my first time here!

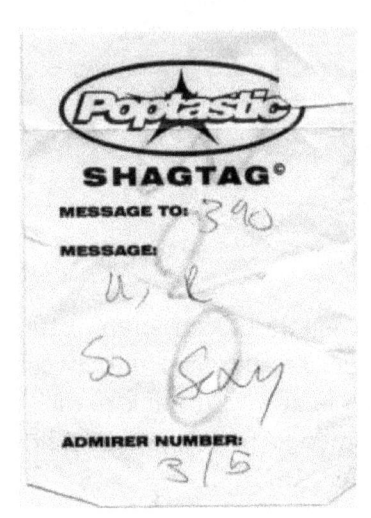

David   *(shouting)* What do you think?

Jon   *(shouting)* It's very busy! Is it always like this?

David   *(shouting)* Ye'! Great, isn't it?

Jonathan wasn't sure…

Jon   *(shouting)* I don't get it. What's the sticker for?

On entering the club every punter's given a sticker with a number on it. This is called a 'Shag-Tag' and if anyone's interested in

---

[92] A vodka-based Alco-pop - a hybrid word for alcohol that tastes like a fizzy soft drink (referred to as 'pop').

'shagging' you they can leave you a message on the 'Shag-Tag Board'.[93] It's all very civilised.

Jon   *(shouting)* A *'Shag-Tag'*!??

David   *(shouting)* Just keep your eye on the board! See if your number comes up!

Jonathan looked over to the board. Kylie was singing *Better the Devil You Know*[94] when it struck him, all the guys were…

David   *(shouting)* I'm gunna check on Charlie. She's been fuckin' ages!

…It was a fucking gay club! And he was alone, and the place was heaving, and everywhere he looked he could see 'gayness'. Why hadn't he realised before? What was he doing here?

Someone brushed past him and he felt his back stiffen. He decided to find a corner. He pulled off the sticky label as he headed for the other room. He hoped it would be quieter. He was wrong. People were all over the place. The music pumped out *Sexy Boy*,[95] and somehow this felt even worse than the Camp Room. And then David and Charlie arrived.

David   *(shouting)* Found you!

Charlie   *(shouting)* David said we know some of the same people!

Jon   *(shouting)* Ye'!

---

[93] In 2003 a new SMS (phone text) service was developed, but it soon went back to the old-style board, as described, within a year.
[94] Or it could have been the Steps cover. He wasn't such an expert on 'this sort of music'.
[95] *Sexy Boy* by The Kinky Boyz, featuring Kia, *(1999)* became an iconic music track after it was used in Channel Four's drama series *Queer as Folk*. (*See* **Further Crippled**)

But he needed to change the subject, or he'd be rumbled.

Jon   *(shouting)* I didn't realise this place was gay!

Charlie   *(shouting)* You never been before?

Jon   *(shouting)* No!

Charlie   *(shouting)* You have a good time! Catch you later!

And with that they vanished into the crowd.

A few beers later, let's say about five or six, Jonathan felt more relaxed in the company of *'others'*. He danced, drank, sniffed something that smelt like old socks and made his heart race, [96] and he was having a great time! And then – like all great times – it came to an end.

The lights came up and the music stopped. The red faced, sweaty punters looked dishevelled, their glamour evaporating quicker than their Poppers. It was 2.40 in the morning, and the place was emptying with a steady flow of shuffling feet.

In light and silence the club lost its magic. It was just another dirty, damp basement, with beer and sweat running down the walls. The illusion vanishing along with its people.

Outside the drunken masses harassed taxis, walking and talking in all directions. Boys and boys, and girls with girl… And some with both, and some with neither. And alcohol and cigarettes. The smell of stale urine and beer hanging in the air. Voices cutting the night with names and insults. This was such a nigh. This was Manchester.

David   You wanna get a taxi back?

---

[96] Poppers – the term given to amyl nitrite (butyl nitrite and isobutyl nitrite) which, when inhaled through the nose, gives you a 'head rush' caused by a surge of blood through the heart and brain.

It was David and Charlie.

Jon   Sure!

And after a good while of black cab spotting they managed to flag one down…

In Manchester it's not so much 'spotting' the cab, it's getting the fucker to take you!

Fifteen or so minutes later they were in Withington,[97] the journey's end, but not necessarily the night's.

David   Wanna come in for a coffee?

Jonathan didn't need to think twice. His head was still buzzing from the club, and he wanted the night to last for as long as he could make it. Charlie gave apologies and carried on in the cab to Didsbury,[98] further down the road.

David put the fire on and told Jonathan to make himself at home.

David   Coffee or tea?

Jon   Tea, please.

David   Milk and sugar?

Jon   Milk, no sugar.

---

[97] Withington is a small village a few miles outside of Manchester City Centre, with a high student population.
[98] Didsbury – another small village, like Withington, but with higher rent prices.

With a quick flick of a remote music appeared. It was Dido, *Here with Me*.

David   *(as he slipped out to make tea)* Change it if you want. There's a stack of CDs down there.

Jonathan sat and listened, gazing around the room, as the tranquil music filtered into his club-muffled ears.

A track later David reappeared with two cups of tea and an opened packet of Hob-Nobs.

David   *(handing Jonathan a cup)* There you go. Help yourself to a biscuit.

And Jonathan did.

           So, what did you think of Poptastic?

Jon   *(with a mouthful of biscuit)* It's good.

David   Went quite a lot last term, too much really... Now I try and keep it to Saturdays. What sort of music do you like?

David was rummaging through his CDs. He had a habit of not putting them back in the cases... So he had to shuffled through the discs like a pack of playing cards, looking for something half-decent to put on.

David   Eminem?

Jon   Sure!

He hadn't got a clue. His mum only ever played Daniel O'Donnell and Neil Diamond.

Eminem became the soundtrack of the night, as they talked and joked, and brought up stories of this and that – and who knows who – and time flew by and the light came in at the window – and it was time to go.

Jon	I should be going.

David	We should do this again sometime.

Jon	Ye'.

And as he rose to leave David gave him a hug and kissed his cheek.

BOOK TWO
The Lover's Book

HAGAL'S AETTIR[99]

The Son, Growth and the Mind.

Chapter One - Disruption

4.33 p.m.   Wednesday, 18th June 2003.

It was a hot summer. One of the hottest on record. You broke out in a sweat just thinking about it. But for Jonathan the day was just the same, if just a lot hotter.

It was seven days after Jonathan's 23rd birthday. I'll skip over the details, as it was pretty much the same as any other afternoon, except for the addition of party hats and a Marks and Spencer's trifle.

Mother entered with a tray.

Mother   Is Jonathan ready for his tea now?

Is he ever bloody ready?

Mother   We'll just put this round in case you spill.

---

[99] Hagal's Aettir (*Hagal - Hagall* or *Hagalaz*) is the second of the three sets of eight runes. (*See* Appendix II)

Which you always do.

As she tied a chequered tea towel around his neck.

Mother   You look just like Jessie James now.

Really?

Mother   Open wide for Mummy.

She must get so pissed off with saying that. It's every bloody meal time - 'Open wide for mummy' - She must realise by now, this is the widest I can get my frigging mouth open.

More food cascaded down his chin and onto the gingham cloth...

Mother   Is that nice?

I don't know. I haven't actually swallowed any of it yet.

He spills more than he bloody eats. You could feed a family on what he spills down his front.

Why don't you just chuck it down my shirt, Mum. It would save us both a lot of time and effort.

Mother   Ooo, we're spilling.

You're spilling. God, I feel like slapping her sometimes.

Come on, eat.

Will you let me eat?

Mother   Are we full?

She stopped shovelling.

Just feed me, will you!

She started again.

Eat you bastard! Eat!

Stop pushing it in. Let me swallow.

He spat out the food to stop himself from choking.

Mother   Don't spit it out, dear. Had enough?

But still she shovels it in.

You keep choking me! Don't feed me so fast. You don't give me time to swallow.

He spits out more food.

Mother   Jonathan! I said to stop that.

Slow down!

All I seem to do is feed him and clean him. All day, every day... Year in, year out... It makes me sick! What sort of a life have I got? What sort of a frigging life!

Mother   Eat, you bastard!

And she slapped him!

In an instant she realised what's she'd done... And so did he. He began to spasm as she held him, hugged him... Tried to comfort the child she didn't even know understood.

Mother   I'm sorry. I'm sorry. Mummy didn't mean it. Mummy's sorry. Oh, I'm sorry. I'm sorry, my darling. I'm sorry.

Jonathan cried the words out in his head.

You bitch! You drunken bitch! Don't touch me. Get off me… Just go away…

***

At his father's funeral. Enid said…

Enid   Maybe you should think about having him put into care. It's too much for you… He needs to be around his own sort…

Mother   He's all I've got left now.

And with that she aged another ten years. After the day of the accident she changed. She became old beyond her years. She lost the fun. It was as though a part of her had died that day. And then – when her husband died – the rest of her died too. Like a hollow shell, in a Marks' cardigan, she dusted and hoovered. Shuffling around the house as though she was a hundred years old. Her spark extinguished. Her life over.

***

School is sometimes the best place for a boy. When you're thirteen and your hormones are just kicking in – it's the best of times and the worst of times – and 'Dick-ins' is on every boy's mind.[100] And every phrase has an innuendo (or in-your-end-hole) – and every word has a double-entendre (I'll leave it up to you to make your own joke up). The school yard becomes the stock exchange of sexual insider dealings (if you know what I mean) brokered by adolescents who

---

[100] 'It was the best of times, it was the worst of times, it was the age of wisdom, it was the age of foolishness, it was the epoch of belief, it was the epoch of incredulity, it was the season of Light, it was the season of Darkness, it was the spring of hope, it was the winter of despair' – (*A Tale of Two Cities*, by Charles Dickens)

buy stock and trade shares with as much compassion as Gekko.[101] But these corporate raiders do it without the threat of a court case. There are no rules in the playground...

Stock is what you have and a share is what somebody else has. The best stock - like livestock - is fit, healthy, with a good coat and an impeccable pedigree. A share in someone else's stock is traded for a share of yours. This would be a date. Stock can fall, however, if the bottom falls out of the market[102] – or it could rise[103] – depending on the nature of the market at the time.

Jonny had good stock and had been dealing with shares pretty well since he was nine – that's when he had his first girlfriend. She was called Michelle – and was pretty fit by nine-year-old standards. It was his first kiss... His stock went up and her's went down... And that's the way of the jungle. Girls are 'slappers' and boys are 'studs' – and so end'eth the lesson in how the market works.

By the age of eleven – when Jonny started high school – his stock was doing well. By the end of Year Eight he was the school equivalent of Microsoft. By Year Ten – aged thirteen – Jonny was 'going public' and 'floating his assets'! In other words, he was ready to 'merge'.

The first time he saw a likely 'business partner' was during the school's sports day. This was one of those annual sporting events where everyone wants to be seen – the school equivalent of Royal Ascot, Henley Regatta and Wimbledon – because this is where the real deals were brokered. This is where you could see your stock rise and fall.

And when Jonny first saw Sarah he knew this was the girl for him.

---

[101] Gordon Gekko was the character played by Michael Douglas in the 1987 movie *Wall Street* (written and directed by Oliver Stone) based on the insider stock-market trading scandals of the mid-Eighties.
[102] If a girl becomes a 'slapper' her share price goes down.
[103] If she 'puts out' on the first date and you bought in early (if you bought in late the price you paid could be more than its worth on the market).

This is their story…

It was Monday, 12th October, 1993.

The place: the school yard.

The weather: wet and cold.

Sarah was with a bunch of girls.

He was playing football. The ball went out of play and smacked one of the less pretty girls in the face!

Jonny ran over to recover the ball. He glanced at the crying girl and grabbed the ball…

Jonny   Sorry.

He said it without even looking. His eyes were fixed on the girl of his dreams!

Jonny   Wanna go out sometime?

Sarah   Okay.

He smiled, turned and ran back to the game…

This is how most romantic meetings happened. Usually, if a boy fancied you, he'd kick a ball at your head or cover you in paint, or something – this is how he gets your attention! Alerting you to his presence… Jonny always tried to do this subtly. After all, he didn't want to go out with a girl with two black eyes, did he? So, Jonny's trick was to get the girl's attention by kicking the ball at her friend – the girl he didn't want to go out with. As you will know, the cliché goes, pretty girls have - by law - an ugly mate. This girl comes in handy for alibis, crying with, and the odd night out. Jonny would use this ugly girl as his target (on the grounds that 'her face already looked like somebody'd kicked a ball at it').

Their first date was 'round town' that Saturday. This involved holding hands and ferocious kissing. In between sucking faces – if not joined at the hands – they were completely oblivious to one another. Looking like Siamese twins who'd had a long-running feud.

Second date – mid-week – usually meant 'the pictures'. The etiquette of teen dating is simple. If you're taking your date to the movies the girl chooses the film;, you each pay your own ticket; the boy buys the popcorn and drinks.

I know this looks unfair on the boys, having to stump-up for snacks, but it is a carefully worked out plan. She chooses the film because it looks as though you care. In reality, if her attention is distracted by the movie you have a chance of getting to 'first base',[104] and what's the point in paying for a movie you want to see if you're going to spend most of the film planning on how you get your arm round her and onto her tits? The popcorn and drink are also useful because they keep her hands busy and stop her from quickly removing yours in the case of a 'going for bust' snatch! You see, rules and etiquette do have their place in society, if you want sexual contact with a female. This also works with more advanced forms of social etiquette.

The third date is Saturday 'round town' again. This involved holding hands (again) and even more ferocious kissing. Oblivion still continues. If you managed to reach 'first-base' over the mid-week movie, you could try adding this to the good-bye kiss at the bus stop at the end of the afternoon. (NB: If you didn't it would probably be inappropriate to grab her tits now – you would have to wait for a movie opportunity mid-week).

Telephone calls will have been held over the past seven days between you and her – and her and everyone who wants to hear about it. Friends – on your side and her side – will now be putting on pressure for you to go further in the 'heavy-petting' stakes.

---

[104] This is an American term for a kiss, but in the North of England it was re-designated as the term for a 'tit-grope'.

Fourth date – mid-week – you visit her house and meet the parents, or go and see a movie. That's if you didn't reach the tit-grab last week. Remember, there are rules to this game.

Meeting parents is tricky. You have to appear charming, polite, trustworthy and innocent. Remember that the goal of this is to be allowed un-guarded access to their daughter. If it's a front-room or kitchen (where you could be disturbed) you'll have to play it very cool, which means you're only trying to get a second invite. If you play your cards right and show immense charm you may be allowed into the girl's bedroom. This raises the stakes of the game. Once in the bedroom show interest in everything she says and shows you – get down to the kissing – repeat 'first-base' and if there is no resistance move to second position.[105]

For Sarah and Jonny this had been progressing steadily for about three weeks. He'd managed the front-room and 'first-base'. This as pretty much the same access he'd been allowed at the movie – until she'd gently shrugged him off. Yet he still saw this as a result, as she hadn't said anything, or make any sort of fuss about it. However, he didn't feel he could repeat the action anytime soon, and there was still no second position or any access to her room, which pissed him off!

Saturday was Halloween. A party had been arranged at a friend's house. It was fancy dress and there was a rumour that parents were going out for the evening. This meant Jonny had to 'up his game' – or be 'left with useless stock' at the end of the night.

Jonny had got to second position with most girls. In the closing months of last year's trading he'd even gone further! This he wanted to be the night of his first merger, and he wanted Sarah for his *mergee*. Now we can all see the problem, Jonny had to work out a 'dodgy-deal'!

---

[105] This is under the shirt, but on top of the bra.

He knew his stock was good and that her shares were high on the market. What he had to do was win her confidence, get her to lower the price of her shares and then bam! He'd be making his mark on the stock exchange once and for all.

The night of the party came. He was dressed as Dracula – looking suave and 'as-cool-as-fuck' – attracting attention in all the right places. He'd nicked a bottle of vodka, from the sideboard on his way out, and was hunting out more booze, at the party, when Sarah arrived. She was dressed in a tight, low cut, black dress and looked 'sensational'. Which meant her shares had risen over 40% and other investors were beginning to speculate on her.

Dracula moved in for the kill.

Jonny   Hi!

He couldn't take his eyes off her breasts.

           You look amazing!

Sarah   So do you.

Jonny   Not like you.

Which, translated, means 'Your tits look huge'.

Jonny   Fancy a drink?

Sarah   What is there?

Jonny had managed to add a couple of cans and a Smirnoff Mule[106] to his alcohol collection. He offered her the choice. She took the Mule.

---

[106] The Smirnoff Mule was the drink that made Pierre Smirnoff famous in America in the 1940s. It is a traditional vodka cocktail base on lime and ginger, and its designer 275ml bottle boasts a shot (25ml) and a half of pure Smirnoff vodka.

In moments they had found a quiet spot in the hallway and were kissing. I say kissing, they were eating one another... I could make a joke about vampires here, but you'd be expecting it, right?[107] Anyway, Jonny went for the 'first-base' and she allowed it.

She didn't shrug him off this time.

Giving it an alcohol content of 5.5% vol. Just enough to get a 'nice girl' – who doesn't drink much – a little bit of Russian-courage when it comes to boys!
[107] Fangs for your support!

The kissing and the vodka were working, and because her dress was cut so low he'd jumped to second position without trying... It was skin on skin and she still didn't mind. Dracula had risen! Know what I mean?

Sarah Can I ask you something?

She could ask what she wanted, but the state he was in she'd be lucky if he could answer it.

Jonny (almost panting) Sure.

Sarah Do you really think I look nice?

She stopped kissing him to ask that?

Jonny (still panting like a dog) 'Course!

He wanted to get back to the 'pre-nuptials' but she stopped him.

Sarah Really?

Jonny Really.

Sarah So if I said you could, would you?

He couldn't believe his ears!

Jonny *(he was knocked for six and stumbled over his answer)* Sure... Ye'... 'course!

He didn't think his dick could get any harder – but it did!

She just smiled and then engaged him in a kiss that nearly sucked out his lower-intestines.

As they kissed Jonny moved his pelvis towards her so she could feel his erection against her. He could sense her smiling through the kiss.

Sarah   Want to go somewhere quieter?

He looked down to his pants.

Jonny   In a minute. I just need to let this go down a bit.

But it didn't…

Sarah   Come on. The coast is clear. I'll go first.

She led him out into the back garden and found the quiet, secluded alleyway where the bin was kept. There was hardly any light. The air was cold. It was damp. But boy, were they hot! Kissing turned into groping. Jonny had his fingers in her. She was wanking him off. But after only a few seconds into it he had to stop her.

Jonny   *(gasping)* Stop! I'm gunna cum.

She stopped – but it was too late!

Jonny ejaculated a bucket-load of cum onto the flag-stones, with a spasm that make his body jerk like he couldn't believe. As he gasped for air Sarah stroked his balls. It was torture – in the most pleasant kind of way.

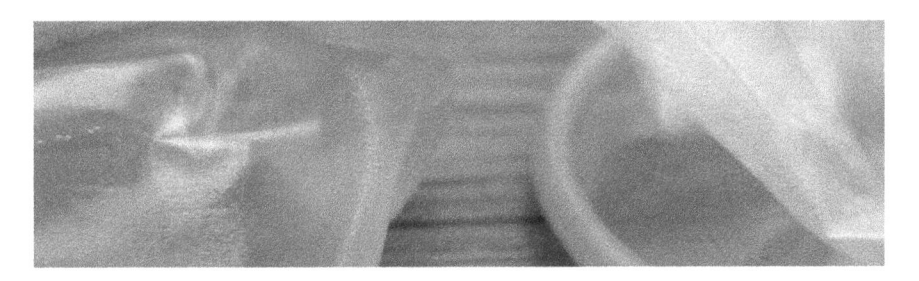

Sarah   Maybe we can try again later.

She started kissing him and before he knew it, he was ready again…

Sarah   Got a condom?

Jonny   Ye'.

He took out the condom – shaking - nervous, excited, frightened – he rolled on the rubber. He could do this blindfold. Although he'd never used one on a girl before, he'd often 'practised' the application of a condom at home in what is technically called 'a posh wank'[108].

Sarah guided him into her body and within seconds he'd cum again... And it was over! He'd merged! He was a player! He was a man!

Jonny always remembered that first time. His first 'real' time. He'd had blow-jobs and hand-jobs before from girls, but never actually fucked one – not until that Halloween – and he knew that life would never be the same again... His stock had risen and her shares (to him) were priceless. She had the three 'P's: pretty, popular and she 'put-out'.

Was she a virgin before that night, you ask yourself? She seemed pretty much in control of the situation. She made the first move. The answer is: 'we'll never know'. All that mattered to Jonny was his stock had risen and so had her share price. Who, if anybody, she'd fucked before him never came to light. As far as anyone knew, she was a virgin – until that night – and they both spread the word of 'the merger' with great pride. They fucked countless times after that, until Jonny was caught doing a secret merger with a rival company three weeks later. There was no stopping him after his first big deal. It was like an addiction.

Sex is an addiction to boys. Before you have it (you want it, dream about it, fantasise about what it will be like – but you manage to live a normal life) everything's okay and then, once you've done it, your mind and body go bonkers. It's like a drug. You always need your next fix. Your next rut!

---

[108] Posh Wank is the term given to masturbating while wearing a condom.

For Jonny – and probably all the boys you'd ever care to ask – the sexual act is about the *sensation*. It's about that release. The pleasant sensation of sticking your dick in a moist, tight hole and ejaculating. It's the fuck, the screw, the shag, the bang, the bonk. It's about cumming, shooting, blowing your load – popping your cork – get your rocks off. It's what defines you. It's the act of being a man.

In school, boys play at being men, as we all play at being ourselves later on. It's no more false – and no more real – than how we all define our natures. We are our actions – and boys fuck girls – that's what they do. That's who they are.

Youth is a time of possibilities, a time when getting pissed feels sophisticated and lipstick kisses feel like 'the real thing' ...

>
> The first love hits without warning
>   and aches your heart
>   and sweats your palms.
> With awkward hands and words
>   you try to make sense
>   of the hormones tearing you apart
>   killing the person you used to be
>   terraforming you
>   into something you can barely control
>   and constantly despise.

Chapter Two - Need

11.48 p.m.   Saturday, 20th June 2003.[109]

Essential night club, on the corner of Bloom Street.

The music pounded out on three floors. Men danced in every available space. Naked torsos of all shapes and sizes gyrated to a rhythm that infused the air. This was a scene from an apocalypse, where every creature in the place had a need to dance. With eyes as wild as beasts, they sweat and gnash their teeth to the thumping sound of a hypnotic trance. This was a gay club. Not pretend like the one before. Not glamorous. Not illusionary. This was real. This was the lair of the follower.. The temple of the god-head. You could feel it. Taste it. Touch it.[110]

David   *(shouting over the music)* What do you think?

Jon   *(shouting back)* It's scary!

David   *(shouting)* Come on!

---

[109] Essential's 3rd Birthday Weekend.
[110] *See* Appendix IV.

David lead Jonathan up a staircase into a packed room at the top of the building. You could feel the heat hit you as you opened the double-doors.

They called it The Pop Lounge.

They fought their way through the dance floor to a seated area, strewn with the bodies of clubbed-out human garbage. Some had tangled themselves together. Their eyes still wild. Their teeth still clenched. Holding on to the music in their heads, as though their lives depended on it. Rocking like orphans. All their faces fixed in the same hypnotic stare.

David	*(shouting)* Is this better?

It was just another layer of Dante's *Inferno*.[111]

Jon	*(shouting)* Ye'! It's fine!

David	*(shouting)* Do you want anything?

Jon	*(shouting)* What?

David	*(shouting)* I said – Do you want anything?

---

[111] Dante Alighieri *(1265-1321)* was a Florentine writer and philosopher who completed a three-volume epic of theology, known as *The Divine Comedy*, in 1308. The first volume of the book is titled *Inferno*, the second *Purgatory* and the final volume *Paradise*. The poem deals with the redemption of man and his ascent into heaven. In the *Inferno* we see the sins of the sinner and the punishment of the damned.

Jon   *(shouting)* What do you mean?

David   *(shouting)* Pills!

Jon   *(shouting)* OK!

Jonathan thought he'd gone to the bar... for Pils.[112]

He hadn't, he'd gone to the toilet... for pills.[113]

David returned – *eventually* – and handed Jonathan a small white pill. He looked at the tablet and then at David, who was knocking his back with a swig of bottled water.

David   *(shouting and handing Jonathan the water)* OK?

Jon   *(shouting)* Fine!

And without a second thought he took the water and kicked back his pill.

Thirty minutes later Jonathan could feel the pill rising in him. He was 'coming up'. It started in the centre of his body, like warm waves washing through him. Each new breaker seeming to waken him inside. Connecting him to the music, and the mood, and the masses of melting flesh around him.

David and Jonathan made their way down to the bottom dance floor.

It was dark – and a sea of skin – greeted them, a living crowd moving as one mass. The undulating, convulsions of a single entity, driven by a single hypnotic drone. In cages, oiled men danced like deities, others gazing on in awe at their perfection. The rhythm was

---

[112] Pils – an abbreviation for Pilsner (or Pilsener) a type of strong bottled lager which originated from Pilsen in Czechoslovakia.

[113] The term given to Ecstasy tablets (also known as MDMA or Es. *See* Appendix IX)

their god's will – and this paradise praised him – as every atom of the universe was fused by it, and to it, and with it.

Deep in the mass of bodies, David and Jonathan danced. Eye to eye in the packed arena they noticed no one, save themselves. In their own bubble of time and space they danced. Hours and minutes meant nothing anymore. Manchester and England melted away, their bodies and thoughts too.

David removed his shirt, wringing wet with his sweat. His skin glistened in the club-light. His perfect body shining, left nipple pierced, with a silver bar, on his arm a tattoo. Jonathan watched as the black, tribal glyph, moved and danced along with them. Its three-dimensional form raised above his shoulder, emitting a black light that twisted, snake-like, weaving itself around them in a cocoon, drawing them closer.

David flung his arms around Jonathan and gave him a hug.

David	*(shouting in Jonathan's ear)* I'm so glad you're here with me.

And they danced, and danced, and danced…

Six a.m. and they left the club into daylight. Eyes squinting. The cold morning air hitting their wet clothes and soggy bodies.

David   We'll get a taxi. There's just something I've got to do first.

And he was gone and back before Jonathan really noticed *he'd went*.

David   OK. Let's get back to mine!

***

At David's they flopped out on the floor. Candles burnt. The curtains holding back the morning light. Holding back the day. Holding in the night.

David   See what I got.

He held up a small bag of white powder, with a smile.

Jon   *(still muggy from the pills he'd taken)* What?

David   K![114] Want some?

Jon   What does it do?

David   Try some and find out.

Jon   OK.

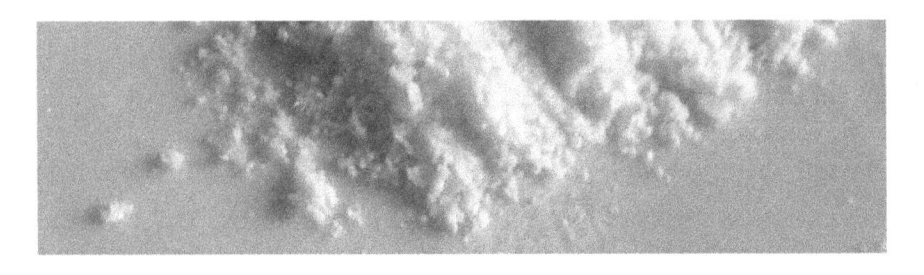

---

[114] K – the abbreviation for Ketamine. An animal anaesthetic. (*See* Appendix X)

Jonathan watched as David tipped the bag's contents onto a large plate; it was as though he was handling gold. Every grain had to be accounted for. Every crystal had to be checked. His concentration and focus was 100% on the job at hand. Then, like a seasoned professional, he took his cash-card from his wallet, and began crunching up the powder and cutting it into neat thin lines, like in the movies. Jonathan felt the butterflies in his stomach, as fear and excitement cut itself into the K.

David   Got a tenner?

Without a word, transfixed by the events unfolding, Jonathan handed David a ten-pound note, which he rolled into a tube.

David   You first.

Jon   No, you first.

David   OK.

Using the rolled-up tenner David snorted up a line of the ketamine. He threw his head back, sniffing and snorting, handing over the note to Jonathan…

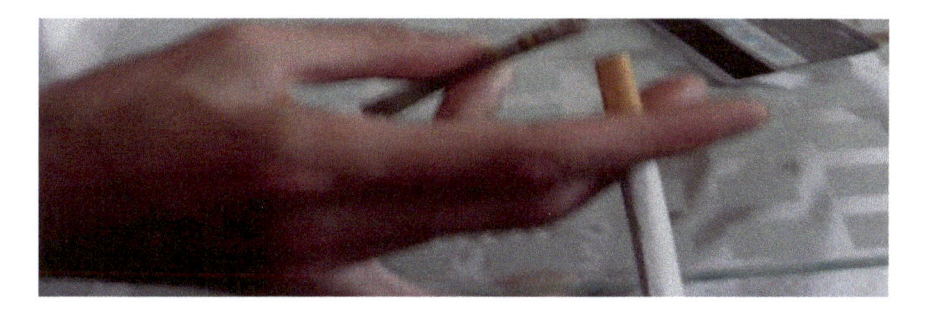

Jon   I've never done this before.

David   Don't worry. Just remember to sniff up – don't blow!

With a deep breath Jonathan hoovered up one of the lines. He could feel the powder at the back of his nose and sniffed. It trickled down the back of his throat. Its taste was bitter. His body juddered in sympathy. It was awful.

David   *(seeing Jon's face)* I'll get you a drink.

David left the room and within a few moments Jonathan could feel himself sinking. He was handed a glass of water – he drank. And then, and then he started to feel heavy. His head was dizzy and he felt a little bit sick – he lay back onto the floor and closed his eyes.

It felt as though his head and body where being tipped back – as though he was mentally falling backwards into himself. He opened his eyes and he could see the room and David and it was the same as before, but different at the same time. There was no time. There was no Jonathan. He was outside of himself - but deep inside – his reality, his fantasy, his dreams and his memories all mixed, confused with the clarity of a vision. He closed his eyes and he was flying over an ancient desert city; the buildings, all pristine and white – geometric – like a circuit board, gleaming white. The sand, the colour of David's skin. And he was in a white room. Egypt. Pure white. Perfect white. A window – thick billowing cotton, tranquil. He would be there for the rest of his life. This is how people go mad. This is how you lose your mind. You fall into this place and never return – and the world thinks you're mad, but really, you're here. In this beautiful, peaceful place. If this is madness – if this is what it's like...

And then... And then... He was back. But he wasn't, he was still there – only different again.

Jon   *(his words slurred)* Who am I?

He seriously had no concept of who he was – but he wasn't frightened. David laughed.

David   *(smiling)* Jon.

He'd seen this sort of thing before with K.

Jon   *(slurred)* Jon?

This didn't make any sense to him.

David   You're in a K-hole.[115]

Jon   *(slurred)* I was flying, like an eagle, or something like an eagle… And this city… I was at the centre of everything and I felt like I wouldn't come back. And then I was mad and I didn't mind because it doesn't really matter… Nothing really matters does it?

David   You're talking bollocks.

David and ketamine had mixed socially for a while and, although he felt a little fuzzy, he was nowhere near as fucked as Jonathan.[116]

Jon   *(still slurring)* It's weird. You look like someone I used to know at school. Your face keeps changing.

David   That's the K.

Jon   *(slurred)* I have so many secrets, and so many things I want to say. And I really want to tell you things, but it's so difficult, like when I see you and everything. It's not real. This is not real. I just imagine it and here you are – but in my head it all feels more real than when I'm actually not imagining it. Do you know what I mean?

David   *(laughing)* No.

---

[115] The term given to a ketamine 'trip'. (*See* Appendix X)
[116] Ketamine has a tolerance level. Every time you take ketamine your tolerance to it rises – thus needing more each time to 'K-hole'. (*See* Appendix X)

Jon   *(slurred)* Look… I imagine stuff, right?

David   OK.

Jon   *(slurred)* I imagined you. You don't really exist. But you do – but just at the bus stop. This is all in my head.

David   You are seriously K'd.

Jon   *(slurred)* I know that for a fact because I can't be here. This isn't me.

David   OK. So, who are you?

Jon   *(slurred)* Me… I'm a fucking cripple.

David   OK.

Jon   *(slurred)* No, seriously. In real life I'm fucking paralysed from the neck down – I'm a fucking quadriplegic, right?

David   If you say so.

Jon   *(slurred)* You're not taking me seriously.

David   I am. I am. I promise.

He didn't want Jon to get all heavy on him.

Jon   *(slurred)* Just because I'm here doesn't make this real… It can't – you can't just make something real by thinking about it, can you?

David   Maybe.

David stroked Jonathan's face and smiled. He thought he was sweet, and he really liked him, a lot.

Jonathan felt as though the fingers had sunk into his skin. The sensation was soft and gentle. More gentle than anything he had ever felt before. No, he had felt it before, something in him remembered it from a lifetime ago. When he was a child. No, when he was a baby. Baby soft, gentle as a baby's touch. Before he knew it, they were both stroking one another. The sensation was like melting and reforming inside one another. Closer and closer, their bodies embracing and holding, touching and stroking. And they kissed. Not innocent kisses, passionate kisses. Wet lips and tongues. The sensation engulfing the whole body in a wave of crashing orgasms. It was like sex without sex. It was like being inside someone, becoming just one person made out of two bodies. Or two bodies made out of one person. He had an erection, but couldn't feel it, or felt he had an erection but didn't. David was holding it, sucking it, the sensation was beyond him. He felt fingers inside – or they could have been just on him. Was he having sex, or was it just in his mind because he wanted it so badly? Was this all just a dream, was this real?[117] He didn't know and he didn't care anymore. For the first time in his whole life he was living in his body, while being outside of himself.

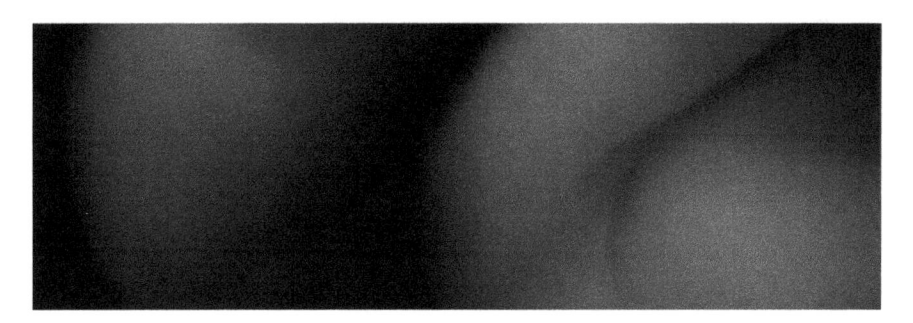

---

[117] Incubus were male demons who are said to have sex with humans while they sleep. Their penises are reported to be ice cold and made of steel.

Chapter Three - Standstill

3:42am   Sunday, 21st June 2003.

Carol was sleeping. Her body twisting and turning like a trapped animal. Sweat pouring from her as she fought her demons deep in her sleep.

***

She remembers winding wool with her mother. Listening to Uncle Mac on the wireless, and a thousand other things – connecting and disconnecting.

He had such a soothing voice, Uncle Mac.[118] *He had a voice like slippers – comfy like the wool. We'd sit round, listening... Winding the wool back from old jumpers...*

Drinking mugs of Bovril[119] – the smell that would remind her of home.

The feeling of them old houses. The way people talked. The way they lived, it's all gone now. It was another world, back then – another time and place.

And it was in that world she met her Bob – they knew that world.

That's what we shared, me and him, our memory of a life that's disappeared.

---

[118] Uncle Mac was Derek McCulloch.
[119] Bovril is the trade name for a beef concentrate used in gravy.

And what now?

Now it's just mine.

And she feels alone. Memories can be such torture.

***

Jonathan woke to the sound of his mother's voice.

Mother	…Wakey-wakey, rise and shine! My you have been a sleepy-head, haven't you? I've been trying to get you up all morning…

He was coming down with the flu. His body ached – or it would have done if he had any feeling in it – and his nose was blocked. Which meant even more doting by Mummy. He hoped she wouldn't notice.

Mother	Let's get you ready. Are you coming down with something? You feel very warm. Have you got the sniffles?

She'd noticed.

Mother	Chicken soup today, I think – and lots of vitamin C!

And with that, he was manhandled into his clothes. She certainly had the ability to put on a cardie in a crisis.

***

David woke up and looked at the clock. He groaned… Another lost Sunday. He thought about getting up and decided not to bother. Instead he would text Charlie, see if she wanted to come round and look after him. He was on a major 'come down' from last night. He ached and his nose was blocked with snot, brought on by the over-indulgence of K.

David texts Charlie.

>   Hi!

Charlie: How woz it?

>   Come round. Just woke up! XXX

And, as if by magic Charlie appeared!

David answered the front door dressed in a bathrobe and what appeared to be a hang-over. Charlie looked at him and made a judgement call.

Charlie   You not up yet, you lazy bastard!?!

David   *(sounding as pathetic as he could)* Didn't get to sleep until one.

Charlie In the afternoon I take it?

David   *(in his most apologetic manner)* Got a bit wasted!

Charlie   *(sarcastically)* Surprise, surprise.

Like it didn't happen every Saturday.

David   I feel like shit.

Charlie   I have no sympathy.

David   Make us a tea, will you?

He tries to look as helpless as he could.

Charlie   Fuckin' great host you are!

He smiled a cheeky smile at her.

David   Couldn't bum a fag off you an' all could I?

Charlie   Anything else?

She throws a packet of Marlboro Lights at him.

David   Love you!

He scampered up the stairs.

Charlie   Sure.

***

In David's room the interrogation began over cigarettes and mugs of tea.

Charlie   So what happened?

David   We went to Essential, left about sixish, came back here, had some K and, he sort of stopped the night.

Charlie's eyes lit up. Gossip! She loved it.

Charlie   *(in excitement)* And?

David   And. *(he was milking this bit)* It was good.

He couldn't help but break out in a grin so big it could have split his face in two.

Charlie   Seeing him again? *(this was almost knicker-wetting gossip)*

David just shrugged his reply.

What does that mean?

She was expecting more of a punch-line.

David   I don't know.

Charlie   What do you mean, you don't know?

This dried her knickers!

David   *(he'd got serious)* I don't know! When I woke up, he wasn't here.

Charlie   Did you get his number?

David gives the pathetic smile of a loser.

Charlie   Why not?

She hated stories with shit endings.

David   I don't know! I was going to ask him in the morning.

Charlie   So, tell me, does he have a big dick?

David   Shut up, you whore!

Chapter Four - Year

10.56 p.m.   Sunday, 21st June 2003.[120]

That night Jonathan listened through the wall as his mother cried herself to sleep. Sometimes it got too much for her.

I want to kill myself. But who would look after him then?

And there she lay alone in her double bed, reaching out for a husband who'd long since gone. Sweat and perfume bleeding from her skin. She'd locked herself back into her dream, hugging the pillow she imagined to be her man.

He might get well again, one day. Mightn't he?

Those hopes have long since gone. The slaughter-house bolt should have come a long time ago.

***

I was brought up to believe that one day you'd get married. And the man you married, he'd look after you, and you'd look after him. Together you'd build a home and have children. Back then you expected different things out of life, it wasn't like it is now. You didn't get choices, you didn't make decisions, things were mapped out for you, you knew where you were. You did your 11+, and if you were bright you went to grammar school, and if you weren't, you went to the secondary modern. One road took you to a career, the other to a job somewhere. And then you got married and had kids.

---

[120] It was the night of the Summer Solstice. A night of changes.

That's all I ever wanted, that Mrs Miniver[121] moment, when you greet your husband home from work and tuck your children up in bed at night, reading them stories, watching them grow up. I'd planned it all out, the wedding, the children, the grandchildren. Roses round the door. And now they aren't here anymore. You invest all your life in them, so much living, for what? Because it didn't turn out, did it? Things happened different. It's like saving money in a biscuit tin under the bed. Thirty years on, it's all worthless. I'm a ten-shilling note in a world of Euros and credit cards. There's no value in what I've saved. If there ever were?

***

Carol never remembered her dreams. Luckily. And the day brought a clean slate to the night. As she hung out the washing, she spied the boy from the bus stop.

He smiled at her and she smiled back, both caught in that moment of 'looking where you shouldn't be'... and wondering if you'd been looking too long not to acknowledge it.

His smile is so sweet – like that of a matinee idol. If I were twenty years younger! I'd still be too old. I don't know if I can ever remember being that young. Being that happy. Having a life that wasn't already pre-destined. Having a smile that didn't hide anything other than 'hello'.

And then he was gone. She looked up the road after him – but he'd vanished. Was he ever there?

***

Nero's, The Triangle, Manchester

---

[121] *Mrs Miniver* was a British movie made in 1942, starring Greer Garson as Mrs Kay Miniver and Walter Pidgeon as her husband Clem. The movie was based on the novel by Jan Struther and won Oscars for best director, best actress, best picture and best screenplay. It is the story of British family keeping 'a stiff-upper-lip' on the home front during World War II.

Charlie   So, did you see him?

David   *(despondently)* No.

She spooned off the froth from her cappuccino and ate it.

Charlie   Look! *(trying to cheer him up)* You had a great time. He knows you like him, and he must like you, or he wouldn't have gone back with you, would he. So all you've got to do is wait. He'll get in touch, I bet you.

David   So why'd he disappear then?

Charlie   I don't know. Some guys are like that.

David   Ye', usually when they've woken up and realised they've made a big mistake.

He looked into her eyes and she could see the hurt.

Charlie   I don't think that's it... Maybe he just had to go and didn't want to wake you up.

David   So why'd he not leave a note? *(he took a deep breath)* He's got a boyfriend, he must have.

She thought the same, but couldn't bear to see him torturing himself.

Charlie   Or a cat?

David   No. Let's face it, he's obviously got someone else. You don't just go like that, unless you've made a mistake.

Charlie   But he did spend the night.

She was clutching at straws for him.

David   He was fucked! By the time he'd had a line of K he could barely remember his name, never mind anything else!

He looked at her. Waiting for her to come up with a plausible argument. She couldn't.

***

That night, as Carol slept, she dreamed about her bus stop boy. She imagined his matinee smile, his beautiful blonde hair, [122] his tanned maple skin, his sensitive, masculine touch…

David   Hi!

She was hanging the washing.

Carol   Hello.

David   *(raising a cigarette as he spoke)* Don't suppose you've got a light, have you?

He smiled and her heart raced.

Carol   Sorry, I don't smoke. *(think, you stupid cow!)* But I might have some matches inside. Come in.

And he followed her into the kitchen, as she looked for the matches.

---

[122] The Flop or Eton Flop, is a male hairstyle that consists of a short back and sides with a long fringe that hangs over the face to cover the eyes. Made popular by the 1920s post-War (that's the First World War *[1914-18]*) aesthetes the, Eaton Flop, is seen as a popular classic cut with many Public School boys, and became widely fashionable in the 1980s after the screening of Granada TV's *Brideshead Revisited*, (broadcast in 1981, in 11 parts, starring Jeremy Irons as Charles Ryder and Anthony Andrews as his 'friend' Sebastian) based on the novel, written in 1945, by the gay writer Evelyn Waugh *(1903–66)*. *Brideshead* is the story of a friendship between two university students during the inter-war years.

Carol   I know I have some somewhere. It's just a matter of finding them. *(she felt herself wittering)* I keep them in case of emergencies. So they should be in this drawer. I keep meaning to sort this drawer out but! You can never find anything when you need it. Here we are!

And there they were – a box of *Swan*. She looked up from her search triumphant, but she wasn't expecting to be dumb-struck. He stood there, bathed in the sunlight – more like an angel than a man, more like a god than a boy. She felt a flush of emotion that nearly dropped her to the floor.

He walked over and gently took the matches from her and as he did so she would swear he lingered. His eyes smiling at her as he said.

David   Thanks!

He put the cigarette to his lips, struck the match and tilted his head. His cupped hands shielding the flame. She couldn't help but be captivated by him. The young, stretched neck. The masculine hands.[123]

Carol   Would you like a drink?

She could see him thinking, and she couldn't allow him to do that.

Carol   Tea? Coffee? Fruit juice?

He was still thinking.

             I have stronger? Gin? Whiskey? I think I might have some vodka somewhere. Brandy? *(she was running out of options)* Water?

David   Tea'll be fine.

---

[123] In her day smoking was still sexy – and here was James Dean 'sparking up' in her kitchen.

He offered back the matches.

Carol   No. You keep them.

David   Thanks.

Carol   Do you take milk and sugar?

David   Ye'. Thanks.

Carol   Take a seat.

What was she thinking?

Carol   Or we could go and sit in the front room. *(this sounded desperate now)* It's up to you.

David   In here's fine.

Of course it was! He probably thought she was a lonely, sad, old woman now!

Carol   Are you a student then?

David   Ye'. I do Art, at the Uni.

Carol   Is that what you want to do?

She avoided adding 'When you grow up' but only just.

David   I'm not sure.

Carol had run out of questions now. She wasn't used to a two-sided conversation. Even Enid didn't really converse like normal people – she sort of talked at you. And anyway, they knew one another. Meeting new people is hard when you've never had to do it before. Bob always met new people, and then they were introduced with a quick, two sentence biog. – "This is Ken, he's married to Monica, and works with me in Finance. Went to the same school as Reg".

As if by instinct Carol had made the tea and arranged a selection of biscuits on a Wedgwood plate.

David Lived here long?

Carol Twenty years. Moved here just after my son was born.

David What does he do?

Piss and shit most of the time.

Carol He…

Did she really want this to define her?

Since 'the accident' that's what she'd become – the poor, sad woman who lives with her spastic son! And she didn't want him to know her like that. She didn't want anybody else to pity her. She didn't want that sorry look – those apologetic words and that sympathetic understanding. She wanted to be herself for once.

Carol He lives abroad. Australia.

Well at least you could have made it plausible, you stupid cow! What if he asks you about it? What the fuck do you know about Australia?

Carol I don't see much of him.

David I went to Australia once.

See! You should have told the truth… Now he's going to think you're a sad 'deluded' old lady… The truth always comes out in the end!

Carol   I've never been... He gets so busy out there.

Great! Now he's feeling sorry for you anyway - only this time it's because your *'made up'* son doesn't give a shit about you... You can't win, can you..?

I must be one of those people who you just can't help feeling sorry for. I might as well have just told him the truth.

David   That's a shame. You'd love it. Golden beaches. The surf.

Carol   It sounds idyllic.

And the way he spoke really did make it sound 'idyllic'.

David   Maybe you should go anyway. Take a trip.

Carol   A trip!

The youth of today! Take a trip indeed – easy for them to say. They just pick up a bag and off they go. At our age you have to think about clothes, passports, sunglasses, jabs, stopping the milk, cancelling the papers (and the window clearer), turning off the electric (and the gas), watering the plants, notifying the neighbours – not mention how it might impact on Christmas. And then there's diarrhoea tablets, barley sugars, Calamine lotion – a whole host of sun products, tea bags, dried milk and Tupperware containers. And that's just off the top of my head. There's things I haven't even begun to think about that need contemplating. People like us don't just go on 'trips' – we arrange the D-Day landings and have 'days out' that need more planning than Dunkirk.

Carol   There's a thought!

David   People should see the world... It really is a beautiful place...

And then she was transported again.

David Sunsets. Cities. Things you've only ever read about, or dreamed of, and there you are, living it, feeling it. The smell of wild jasmine. The taste of fresh cut mango. The sound and feel of waves crashing on a faraway beach. Or the warm monsoon rain washing away the dust of a thousand troubles.

Carol Have a custard cream.

***

And in her dreams Carol smiled.

 A gentle word
   Enough to feel the spring again
   to bask in the sun
   and be brought back from the edge of winter...
     his warm touch melting away the cold
     thawing the thought of what might be
     It's what dreams are made of...
     honeyed by the bees with hidden stings
     and memories of what summer brings
       to feel that sun once more
       and feel the warmth of love blister again.

Chapter Five - Defence

9.38 a.m.   Tuesday, 23rd June 2003.[124]

As Carol cleaned her son, she remembered the night before.

***

It's not him there. It sounds silly, but it's not him. He just sits there. His eyes look a you, but they don't see. He just stares into space most of the time. I don't even think he knows who I am.

***

I dreamed about the bus stop boy last night.

***

And then she was done. And he was clean. And then she left... and they were then both free to dream.

***

Jonathan was walking down Oxford Road when he saw David, coming up the other way. He smiled.

David   Hi! Didn't think I'd see you again after the other night.

Jon   Why?

---

[124] Midsummer Eve.

David	Well, one minute you were there, and then next…
Jon	Ye', sorry about that. I had to get back.

He could see an excuse coming a mile off… He'd given enough.

David	*(disappointedly)* Ye'.
Jon	No. It's not that. I had a great time, but I live at home. It's my mum, see…
David	And she doesn't know you're 'Out'?[125]
Jon	She knows that! It's just the hassle I get if I stay out all night.
David	*(feeling better already)* So we're still cool?
Jon	Totally.

In fact, he couldn't understand what the problem had been to start with.

David	So will I see you out tonight?
Jon	I'm not sure.
David	Oh, come on – it's Poptastic.

Jonathan thought about it. Let's face it, where else did he have to go?

Jon	OK.

---

[125] 'Out' is an abbreviation for 'out of the closet', the euphemism used to describe people who don't hide their homosexuality from others.

David   Great! Why don't you come to the LGB – then you can get in for nothing. I'll sign you in.

Jon   What's the LGB?

David   The LGB LGB at the Uni.

Jonathan pulled his face of non recognition.

David   The Lesbian, Gay, Bisexual Society. It's part of the Student Union. We meet there before we go down to The Village.[126]

It was as though someone had just hit Jonathan with a hammer.

Jon   You're gay?

David   *(bemused)* What?

Jon   Look I've gotta go. I said I'd meet someone. I'll see you.

And with that he disappeared down Oxford Road.

***

Jonathan's head was spinning. It wasn't supposed to be like this. This was his world. It was in his head. He made it how he wanted it.

---

[126] 'The Village' is the term given to Canal Street, Manchester's gay quarter.

So why'd he make it like this? Why'd he make his best friend a queer?

He thought back to the night in David's flat. The feelings he'd had while he'd been 'fucked-up' on the K… And those amazing, 'trippy' dreams – like he was having sex, floating on the clouds above him, and the sensations of touch – and how he'd felt.

But none of it was real. This was his mind all 'fucked-up' on ketamine, but that wasn't real either… So, if none of it was real, why'd he invented it for himself? Why that experience? Why that fantasy? Was he queer? It didn't bear thinking about.

***

At David's flat.

Charlie *(with haste in her voice)* I came round soon as I could.

She dumped her bag on the bed and gave David her full-on 'concerned' face.

        So, what happened?

David   I saw him.

Charlie   And? *(he just shrugged at her)* What's that mean?

David   I don't know… He just went off on one.

Charlie   What did you say to him?

Obviously it was something he said.

David   I just asked him if he wanted to come to the L.G.B and he freaked!

Charlie couldn't understand this either.

Charlie	Maybe he's not 'Out' yet.
David	He is – I asked him. His mum knows and everything! It was just when I said I was gay he freaked!
Charlie	I thought you said it was when you mentioned the L.G.B?
David	*(looking frustrated)* It was. Then he asked me if I was gay and legged it!
Charlie	Are you sure he's gay?

David looked at her as though she was simple.

David	We met in Essential and I fucked him up the arse – what more evidence do you need?
Charlie	OK, stupid question. *(she'd run out of options)* Well I don't know. Maybe he's just a psycho! Or one of those straight guys who fucks gay men!

Either way, it wasn't looking hopeful for a reunion.

***

Why would I make-up a life like this, when I could make-up anything I wanted? Why would I choose to be a queer? Am I gay? Is that who I really am? Is that why I did it? Deep down inside – am I a queer?

***

He found himself in a bar. He ordered a drink. Across the room he saw an attractive girl, in her early twenties. He knew she was attractive. He knew he fancied her, so how could he be gay?

***

Whitworth Park Halls of Residence was hidden behind a row of dismal little shops, opposite the hospital, in a leafy compound of grotty little buildings resembling a clapped-out old holiday camp.[127] The breeze-block rooms were small and clinical. Just big enough for the small wardrobe, table and single bed. She offered a coffee.

Jon   I'm fine.

Girl   Music?

She put on a sexy *R'n'B* tune and pulled the curtains closed. Which made little difference, the material was so thin.

Girl   I'll just lock the door, so we don't get disturbed.

And by the time she'd returned her T-shirt was off and he was lying on the bed being covered by her kisses. If his subconscious was gay his body certainly wasn't. And within minutes he was fucking her.

***

In the evening, when the house was quiet, Carol and a bottle of red wine would muse.

---

[127] Stalag 17.

Is this me? Is this all I am? All I have? Just memories of a life that's over. Memories of a time gone by - and a future I hardly dare to predict for myself.

She was jolted from her melancholy by a sound she couldn't place. The heating wasn't on so it wasn't that, maybe it was Jonathan? No. It was probably just the house settling itself down for the night... And there it was again. Outside in the garden. Gingerly she eased back the curtain to 'twitch her nets'.[128] And there – bathed in orange street-lighting – was a face she recognised. It was her bus stop boy. Her heart fluttered a little and she felt a blush appear.

What am I thinking? This is stupid. Utterly. Utterly stupid. He's nothing more than child. And me. Who'd look at me? Why am I even thinking like this?

She moved away from the window and retreated into the middle of the room with her glass. But her mind wouldn't rest. And her imagination surged with a hit of alcohol.

The doorbell rang, and Carol's heart jumped into her mouth.

It couldn't be...

Through the glass panel in the door she could see the distinctive outline of her bus stop boy. She smoothed her hair and straightened her skirt as she approached the door. One last check in the mirror before answering – eyes, teeth, hair. And the shape starts to shift – he's going.

Carol   Yes...

As she opened the door with a fake mixture of smiles and surprise.

        Hello...?

---

[128] The art of peeping out of net curtains – perfected in suburbia and other middle-aged enclaves.

David   Hi! I…

He stops.

He's embarrassed.

David   I'm sorry…

He runs his hand through his hair and turn away from her.

Carol   What is it?

David   I didn't know where else to come…

She opened the door wide.

Carol   Come in.

He looked strange in the front room. Like he didn't fit somehow. Like, maybe, he was too young for the patterned wallpaper, or too handsome for the couch.

Carol   Sit down. Would you like a glass of wine?

David   *(giving a nervous smile)* Thanks!

She went to get him a glass from the kitchen. When she returned, he was holding a photograph of Bob and her.

David   Is this your husband?

Carol   Yes. He died a little while ago.

Why did she say that?

David   I'm sorry.

Carol   You get by. *(she sighed)*

She needed to change the subject. This was heading for a major depressive.

Carol   But I'm sure you didn't come to talk about that.

She pours him a glass of wine.

David   *(looking into the glass)* No…

Now he was here, he felt reluctant to talk. But just being there was comfort enough.

Carol   You don't have to talk if you don't want to.

But he felt as though he should at least explain why he'd turned up so dramatically.

David   *(still focusing on the contents of his glass)* I just needed to be around somebody. Things get to me sometimes. You know?

He looked up and saw Carol's sympathy. Guilt ran through him.

David   *(rising from he couch)* Look, maybe I should be going.

Carol   You don't have to. I understand how it feels.

In fact, she could write a book on the subject.

David   I just feel a bit stupid.

Carol decided to take charge.

Carol   Well don't! Anyway, you're here now – and I could do with the company just as much as you. So, let's drink to company!

David   *(raising his glass)* To company!

And for the first time since he arrived, Carol saw a smile hatch across his face. They talked well into the night. Drinking, laughing, joking, and having the best time she could remember in what felt like forever. For a moment she felt twenty-one again.

>Rescued by touch
>the body and hands
>of a half-remembered life
>melting away the years
>welcoming it back
>for good or bad
>its worth everything it might cost.

Chapter Six - Initiation

10.32 a.m.   Wednesday, 24th June 2003.

Carol's morning ritual of washing and cleaning began late. Her head pounding from the wine she'd drunk the night before. But Jonathan still needed 'doing'.

God, my head! I'll have to have a lie down after this.

And she looked at the helpless figure, her own flesh and blood.

Just look at him, the poor love. His thoughts are a million miles away.

And then...

I wish he were dead.

But that only lasted a few seconds before the guilt got to her, and she felt wicked. A thought with no one to share it with. A thought that sent the blood cold.

They all think I'm a saint, down at the church.

If only they could read her mind.

Mother   There you go. Who's a handsome lad?

The boy at the bus stop, that's who.

And the wash is finished. Now all she has to do is feed him.

Mother   Are we sleepy still?

I don't know why, all he ever does is sleep, eat, shit and fart.

Mother   Ready for breakfast?

Here she goes again.

Mother   And this time Mummy promises not to lose her temper.

So, what are you going to choke me with today?

Mother   How does a nice dippy-egg, with soldiers sound?

It sounds marvellous. Not only do I get choked. I now also run the risk of contracting food poisoning as well. Thanks, mum.

Mother   I thought you'd like that.

Yes, and we all know what thought did.[129] *I know, I'm an ungrateful little bastard. If I were her I'd have put me in a Home years ago — but she won't. It's the Christian ethic. Not that she's over religious, because she's not. But she tries and that's the main thing. Anyway, it keeps her busy. If it hadn't been for me and the booze, she'd have gone mental — she's not far off now!*

---

[129] *...it followed a muck cart because it 'thought' it was a wedding!*

I wonder if the bus stop boy will be back today?

She picks up the cold egg from the tray and begins the arduous task of feeding him.

Chapter Seven - Protector

10.45 p.m.   Thursday, 25th June 2003.

Jonathan looked at the clock. He thought about his nights out with David in The Village.

So it's a gay club. So what? Just because I decide to go there doesn't mean I'm gay. And what if he is like that, does it matter?

And before he could stop himself, he was there. In Cruz 101.

Cruz was the club down from Poptastic. And the only place open on a Thursday night.[130] It was busy. For hardened clubbers the weekend started here. He wandered around for a while nursing a bottle of Reef, looking for David in the crowd. And then he saw him. He was kissing another guy. Jonathan felt his stomach somersault. He looked away. He couldn't believe it – he was jealous.

Man   *(shouting over the music)* Hello?

Jonathan smiled.

               …You here with anyone?

Jon   *(shouting back)* No.

Man   *(shouting)* My name's…

But he couldn't quite hear over the noise. The Man offering his hand. Jonathan politely shook it – his attention still on David and his snogging.

Man   …And you are?

Jon   *(shouting)* Jon!

Man   *(shouting)* Jon?

Jon   *(shouting)* Ye'!

Man   *(shouting)* You from Manchester then?

Jon   *(shouting)* Ye'!

Man   *(shouting)* Student?

Jon   *(shouting)* Ye'!

---

[130] Although Poptastic is now open on a Thursday evening.

And then he realised what was happening, he was being chatted up!

Man   (shouting) I'm here with…

Jonathan stopped listening. He was just looking at David and the guy he'd picked up. He noticed the man had stopped talking. He made his apologies and headed for safety, or at least what he thought was safety. The toilet was white, bright and full of men waiting for the cubicles. Like Pavlov's dogs,[131] every time the door opened, they turned their heads. It was a meat market. Jonathan went to the urinal. He was ready to piss – and felt the world was waiting. The guy next to him was looking at his dick. He caught Jonathan's eye.

The Guy   (with a smile) Nice.

And he was then aware of another guy to his left wanking himself off. Jonathan put his dick away and left.

And as he was leaving who should be bump into, but David. He gave Jonathan a piercing look as he walked past him. Jonathan waited.

In what seemed like forever David emerged. Without so much as a second glance he carried on walking.

Jon   (shouting after him) David! Wait!

Jonathan hurried after him. Grabbing his arm to stop him.

David   (pissed off) What?

Jon   I want to explain.

David had heard it all before. He was just another one of those serial 'one-nighters' – Find 'em, Fuck 'em, Forget 'em.

---

[131] Ivan Pavlov *(1849–1936)* was a Russian psychologist who discovered the conditioned reflex. He trained dogs to expect food when a bell rang. After a few months he found that the dogs would salivate when hearing the bell – this was a conditioned reflex.

David   No need. I get the picture.

He started to walk away again.

Jon   Please… It's not what you think.

David   Mind-reader now, are you?

To be truthful David didn't know what to think – but sarcasm is always the best form of defence for a poof!

Jon   I came here looking for you.

David laughed to himself. That was one of the oldest lines in the book – next to 'of course I love you' and 'No, of course I won't cum in your mouth'.

David   Well, now you've found me. Happy?

Jon   I still want us to be friends.

It was as though he'd swallowed a dictionary of clichés.

David   Sure! Whatever.

He started walking off again.

Jon   *(stopping him from leaving)* I didn't mean to hurt your feelings. I didn't realise.

David   You didn't realise what?

Jon   That you were gay. I didn't know how to deal with it. I'm sorry.

David   You're having a laugh, aren't you? You didn't know I was gay? Hello!

He looked around the club, as if to prove that his surroundings over the past few weeks should have alerted him to the 'possibility' that he might have been at least 'a little bit' bent.

Jon — OK, I should have guessed.

David — Guessed. Are you real?

Yes, he really was that naïve.

Jon — I said I was sorry. It's not something I deal with every day.

David — What? So you're telling me that you're 'straight' now, are you?

He was just taking the piss now!

Jon — Yes.

David — So Saturday night, Sunday morning, didn't happen then?

Jon — I don't know what you mean?

David — *(walking away again)* Course!

Jon — *(holding him back)* David!

David — Look! Just leave it, aye!

And with that – he was fuming – he walked off, back to his 'man'.

***

It was past two in the morning and Jonathan had had more alcohol than he could cope with. He was waiting across the road from the club in a doorway - half leaning and half slumped. He was waiting to see David, who emerged with his new flame.

Jon　　　　　*(calling over to him)* David! We need to talk!

He lunged forward to meet him. David just carried on walking.

David　　　　We've talked enough!

Jon　　　　　I said I was sorry. What more can I do?

David　　　　Just leave it.

Jon　　　　　No!

David's Man　He said, leave it!

Jon　　　　　I'm not talking to you.

David's Man　Oh, yes you are!

Jonathan squared-up to a man not as drunk as he was.

David　　　　*(to the man)* Come on.

And they started to walk away.

Jon　　　　　*(shouting at the top of his voice)* David! David!

David　　　　*(to the man)* Look, I'm gonna have to speak to him. Sorry.

David's Man　*(understandingly)* I'll wait here.

David went back to where Jonathan was balancing. He wasn't a happy bunny.

David　　　　*(with venom)* What!?

Jon   *(slurred)* I'm drunk.

David   *(sarcastically)* Tell me something I don't know.

Jon   *(slurred)* I waited for you.

David   So what was all that about the other day. And in there tonight? I don't know what I'm supposed to do. What do you want?

Jon   *(slurred)* I want to be your friend.

David   Right. You're my friend. Now good-night.

He starts to leave.

Jon   *(slurred, with a hint of disappointment)* No. Not like this!

His voice was whining and pathetic.

Jon   Like before. Get rid of him. We're mates.

David   It doesn't work like that!

And with that he walked away.

Jon   *(slurred, calling after him)* David! David!

But David didn't turn back. He carried on walking away.

As David left the car park with his *'shag'*. Jonathan felt his heart knot.

Chapter Eight - Wholeness

2.46 p.m.   Friday, 26th June 2003.

It was afternoon feeding at the zoo. Mother had prepared the animal and now it was just a case of getting it down Jonathan's throat!

Mother   That boy from the bus stop's outside again.

I know.

And then he began to think about the night before.

It's just a fantasy, and I can fantasise about anything I want.

Sometimes the only way to get rid of temptation is to give in to it. To have the courage to live a fantasy. To live a life less ordinary.

I feel like I'm stood on the edge of something – too afraid to jump. The fear of falling, of leaving everything – and everyone – that's safe, and secure, and familiar.

Inside the skull there is another universe.

***

The attraction of a body in motion. The poetry of movement. The unison of muscles, balance and control. The primal link between the hunter and sexual ability. The attraction of the genetic formula that make the body, the desire of it, the want to own it, the admiration of its ability – the admiration, the want and the desire to be, want, own, that body, ability, individual.

***

Basically, we coveted bodies for sex, so we can have their genetic make-up melt with ours – or we copy them, to have the attributes coveted for sex. What if we could experience the body in both ways – by being it and fucking it? The total experience of being giver and receiver of the same body. Like fucking yourself, in the way you want to be fucked – giving yourself pleasure in the way only you know how? Wouldn't this be anybody's dream and fantasy? But does it have to be a fantasy?

***

In the universe of the skull we can be who we want to be. Fuck who we want to fuck!

In the sexual act we can live in another body – use it, be it, experience it. In our skulls we can create worlds without morality – make and remake ourselves by our thoughts – perpetually free to be who we want to be. Our shadow-self – the self we hide in the shadows of our subconscious, the self we hide from everyone, even ourselves at times.

To be with your shadow. To be with it totally. To give in to its desires and emotions, and then to seek out that other shadow. . The Double.[132]

---

[132] *The Double* is another term given to soul-mates or life-partners.

***

And in that moment, he decided to follow the adventure.

Mother   Ooo, we are eating well this afternoon. Do you like dippy-egg?

Mummy does!

He hadn't noticed, and the egg had slipped down without any fuss at all.

BOOK THREE
The Mortal's Book

TIR'S AETTIR[133]

The Soul, Death and the Holy Spirit.

Chapter One - Warrior

3.47 p.m.   Saturday, 12th July 2003.

Carol heard the door bell.

Nobody calls at this time.

It was David with a bunch of flowers.

Carol   Hello.

She felt her heart skip.

David   Hi! *(slightly embarrassed)* I brought you these.

Carol   *(taking the flowers and sniffing them)* Thank you, they're lovely. But you shouldn't have.

---

[133] Tir's Aettir (*Tiu – Tir* or *Teiwaz*) is the third of the three sets of eight runes. (*See* Appendix II)

David   I wanted to.

Carol   Come in. I'll go and put these in water. Make yourself at home.

David went into the living room and sat down.

Carol   *(from the kitchen)* Would you like a drink?

David   *(shouting back)* Thanks.

Carol put the kettle on and returned to her guest.

Carol   So! What have you been up to?

David   *(shrugging)* Nothing much. You?

Carol   You know, same old thing.

This conversation was going nowhere.

Carol   The flowers are lovely. Thank you. It's a long time since anyone bought me flowers.

David   I just wanted to say thank you…

Carol   What for?

David   *(shrugging)* Being there, when I needed you.

Sometimes depression sits on him, hangs over him like a cloud. He can feel it sinking in to his body like damp on the wall and he can't dry it out. It just seeps in; every pore, every part of him hung with the weight of it.

That's when he walks – when he visits the city, at night, alone. Just walking, thinking, the damp following him like a big, black dog hunting after him through the dark.

Carol Let's see if that kettle's boiled.

She needed to get out of there, before she got carried away with herself.

David I was going to come round sooner, but…

Carol That's all right, it's nice to see you whenever.

She was trying to stop her imagination running away with itself. But he wouldn't let her return to the kitchen.

David I don't mean like that.

So she waited to hear what he did mean. Her heart was now doing more than just skipping - it was beating like a tom-tom in the base of her throat. She knew this wouldn't be a *'Mills and Boon'*,[134] but she couldn't help seeing herself as Cathy and him as her Heathcliff.[135]

David That night I came round, [136] when we talked, I thought about it a lot, about *you* a lot. *(his tone changes)* I'm sorry, this is stupid, I should go.

He stands and Carol panics.

---

[134] Mills and Boon are a publishing company that specialise in formulaic romantic fiction. Published in 26 languages, the company's global sales reach around 175 million books a year (with 13 million sold in the United Kingdom alone). It is estimated that around 50 million people read Mills and Boon titles (800 new ones are published each month) making them the biggest publishers in the romantic fiction genre.

[135] Heathcliff (the main characters in the novel *Wuthering Heighs*, written by Emily Bronte *[1818–48]* and first published in 1847 under the pseudonym Ellis Bell). Cathy and Heathcliff's relationship has now passed over into folk-lore, and is often sited as one of the great romances of all time, quite often by people who are completely unaware of its dark context.

[136] 19 days ago.

Carol   David! Please.

She halts his retreat.

Carol   Don't.

David   I should never have said anything.

Carol   I don't understand what you mean.

And that was genuine. She really didn't get it.

David   *(very sheepishly)* It's you.

There was a silence that only he could fill.

David   I can't stop thinking about you. And I know it's daft – why would someone like you want to be with me.

She could think of lots of reasons. His Paul Newman eyes, his matinee smile, his lovely blonde hair. And that was just off the top of her head.

Her heart was pounding – *Mills & Boon, Mills & Boon, Mills & Boon...*

Carol   *(coyly)* I'm flattered. I don't know what to say.

David   I should never have said anything.

There was another one of those expectant pauses.

David   I've embarrassed you.

Carol   No! It's just a shock.

David   I'll go.

Carol   No. Please. Sit down. I just don't know what to say.

Carol had spent most of her adult life with one man. She had only ever been 'courted' by one man, the man she married, and remained faithful to for over twenty years, and the prospect of dealing with 'suitors' was daunting.

David   It's my age, isn't it?

It wasn't just that...

But that was one of the reasons that made him so damn attractive.

Carol   ...I've been on my own for such a long time now.

This sounded like a 'thanks', but 'no thanks' moment...

And Carol felt herself putting duty before desire. To do the right thing and talk him out of her life.

Carol   ...It's just a bit of a shock...

David   I understand.

She'd defused the situation. It was over. Her one minute of temptation had been overridden by her motherly instinct to protect him from the clutches of an older woman. Even if the older woman was her. She felt a deep sigh release inside her.

But was it relief or regret?

Carol   I'll go and make that tea.

She retreated into the kitchen, and a smile engulfed her, radiating from her like sunlight, filling the room with a feeling that made her feel alive again, and she thought,

What if...

Carol returned with the tea and placed it on the coffee table.

Carol   You know this can't happen, you and me.

David   I know.

Carol   It would be wrong.

David   Why? Why does it have to be wrong!

Carol   Because you're too young. It just wouldn't work.

David   You don't know that.

Carol   I do. And you do to.

David   Not if we wanted it.

Carol   And what would people say?

David   I don't care what people say!

Carol   But I do. What about my friends? Your friends? It wouldn't work.

David   But I love you.

Carol   You think you love me.

David   I know what I feel.

Carol was drawn to his soulful eyes and his begging expression. The motherly instinct had packed its bags and gone south for the winter.

Carol   Do you?

David   Let me prove it.

And with that he bent forward and kissed her gently upon the lips.

His soft lips left their ghost as he lent back to look at her.

Carol   We shouldn't be doing this.

He lent forward and kissed her again, this time their lips parting, their tongues engaging. The passion stoking as they closed their eyes, falling into the moment, tumbling through a million desires and emotions as they lost themselves in the action.He lent forward and kissed her again - this time their lips parting - their tongues engaging - the passion stoking as they closed their eyes - falling into the moment - tumbling through a million desires and emotions as they lost themselves in the action.

Carol   No!

She broke away from the kiss and looked at him.

Carol   You're too young.

She was scared of so much.

David   I'm old enough to decide that for myself.

Carol   This isn't about you. It's about me.

It was like kissing her son. Like kissing a child. She felt dirty. Even in her dreams she couldn't bring herself to be free!

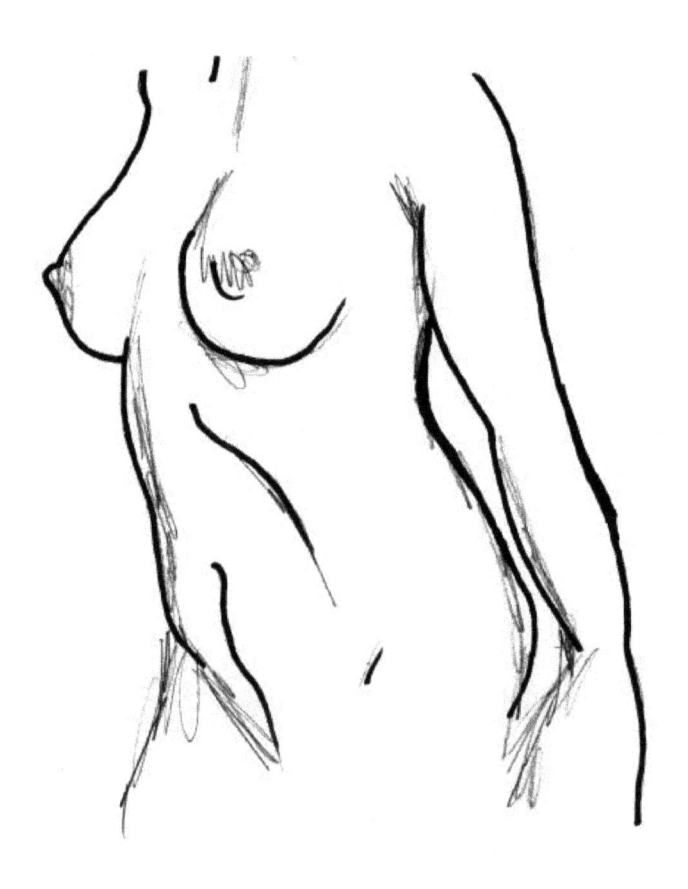

David's Sketch of Carol

***

Jonathan sat in Via Fossa[137] nursing a Diet Coke. It was late afternoon and the bar was starting to get busy with people 'having one after work'. He was here to see - see if he could - see if he really could 'do it' …

---

[137] One of the bars on Canal Street (*Via Fossa* being Latin for Canal Street).

Guy			Anyone sat here?

He resisted the crappy one-liner 'if there is then they're very small' and just said…

Jon			No, it's fine.

Then there was silence. In fact, the guy had turned away from him altogether. Of course, he didn't know what to expect, but this was just like any 'normal' pub and he was just sat next to a 'normal' stranger.

He felt a bit stupid. He expected it to be more like the club. He expected the chat-up lines. He expected to be looked at. He expected too much!

He drank his Coke and went out onto the street.

It was warm and people were sat at tables, watching the world float by. It was the way Jonathan imagined Paris would be. He lent against the wall and felt the sun on his face. He thought about David and how nice it would be to share this with him, and then…

Another guy	On your own?

Jon			What?

Another guy	On your own?

Jon			*(cagey)* Ye'?

Another guy   Mind if I join you?

He lent on the wall beside him.

        The name's Darren.[138]

Jon   Jon.

Darren   Student?

Jon   Ye'.

Darren   Haven't seen you around here before.

There was a pause in the questioning.

        Can I get you a drink?

Jon   No, you're alright.

Darren   I know, but that's not what I asked.

The joke was feeble, but it made Jon smile.

Darren   So, what do you wanna drink?

Jon   *(smiling)* Diet Coke.

Darren   Ice and lemon?

Jon   *(still smiling)* OK.

Darren disappeared into the bar.

Is this how it happens? Is this what gays do?

---

[138] Dark hair. Late twenties, early thirties. Muscular build. Fashionably-Manchester looking.

He could feel the butterflies in his stomach. He was doing it. He was finally starting his adventure.

Darren   *(with a Diet Coke)* There you are!

Jon   Cheers!

Darren   Do you wanna sit down? There's a table over there.

Jon   OK.

They sat.

Darren   So. Tell me about yourself. What do you do, when you're not out here looking gorgeous?

Jon couldn't help his embarrassment at the overt compliment.

Jon   Medicine.

Darren   Brains as well?

Jon   And you?

Taking a sip from his Diet Coke.

Darren   I.T.[139]

Then there was a gap.

So, are you seeing anyone?

He could still escape if he wanted to. This would be the ideal 'get-out' clause… If he wanted to. He still had a choice of whether to go through with this or not.

Jon   No, and you?

---

[139] Everyone in The Village over 25 seems to be in I.T (Information Technology).

He cut the safety rope.

Darren   Not at the moment.

This was it. This was what he wanted – wasn't it? It must be. This was his fantasy after all.

Darren   So, what are your plans for today?

Jon shrugged and pulled a face – the international gesture for 'nothing much'.

Jon   You?

This was a dance – a waltz. Darren leading and Jon picking it up pretty quickly for a Village-novice. But we'll cut to the chase…

Darren   Fancy coming back to mine for a while? Let me get chance to shower and change, then we can hit town.

Jon   OK.

Jon half knew what was going on. Or he thought he had a good idea of the strategy.

Looking for animals
   strayed from different parts
   unaware with endocrine lurking
      His sighs wormlke
      he thinks in two main parts
      In the dark nervous
         Peripheral
         Central
      You can almost feel his brain
         his spinal cord
           Breathless
           Bundles

> He shows fibres that connect
> > alone
> transmits signals
> for the moment
> the brains calls kiss
> > to fuck with the light on
> and the safety off
> a cigarette lit
> a passion sparked.

***

Darren's apartment was near to The Village in a converted Victorian building. Once these buildings had been the warehouses and offices of the cotton trade. Now they were some of the most desirable properties in Manchester.[140]

Darren   Make yourself at home!

The flat was an open-plan room with white walls and exposed brickwork. The floor – laminated. The furniture – IKEA. Just like every other aspiring middle-class gay abode in Manchester.

         Drink?

Jon   What you got?

---

[140] Probably some of the best properties North of Watford.

Darren		Tea? Coffee? Beer? Wine?

Jon		Beer'll be fine.

He needed the Dutch courage!

Darren		*(handing Jon a beer and flopping down on the sofa beside him)* So, what do you think?

Jon		*(looking around the room and swigging the beer)* Nice.

Darren		*(stroking Jon's arm with his finger)* Like you then.

And before Jon knew it the Budweiser was on the coffee table and they were eating one another's faces off. Jon's eyes were tightly closed as he tried to talk himself into the experience. His face being stung by Darren's stubble *(that seemed to have come from nowhere to exfoliate his face)* and his hands. They seemed to be everywhere at the same time. He felt mauled. The pressure of Darren's lips against him – the grasping hands and rasping breath. He pulled away.

Darren		*(out of breath)* Are you OK?

Jon		*(not sure)* Ye'! I'm fine.

Darren		*(eagerly)* Wanna go into the bedroom?

Jon		*(still not sure)* OK.

He needed to do this, to get it over with, to know for sure.

***

The bedroom was another cloned IKEA 'serving suggestion'. White, oatmeal and exposed brickwork, paper light shades and laminated flooring, the obligatory black and white photos in clip frames.

They say that gay men are very imaginative and artistic... Until it comes to interior design, it seems. It's as though gay men are hard-wired to replicate a standard bedroom decor. This may be caused by promiscuity – and the usefulness of a 'standard' bedroom layout to avoid confusion in a stranger's house when it's dark or you're pissed off your face.

Jon didn't have time to notice much. His eyes were tightly shut again as they resumed their previous entanglement.

With experience comes technique.

Before he knew it, his shirt was undone – and off. Then, as if by magic, Darren had somehow managed to unzip his jeans and was now in the process of sucking him off. But it was all too quick, he wasn't hard yet, nor could he get hard, a few minutes passed.

Jon *(embarrassed)* Sorry.

Darren *(looking up at him)* That's OK.

But it wasn't, Darren would have to resort to foreplay, which meant more kissing and some heavy groping. This fantasy was quickly turning into Jon's worst nightmare.

Darren stopped for a breather.

Jon *(apologetic)* I'm sorry, I should go.

Darren *(pretending to care)* No. Don't be silly. Just relax, it's no big deal.

Which we all know is short-speak for: *'You're not fucking coming in here and getting me all fucking worked-up just so that you can have your dick sucked and then piss-off without doing me'*.
Darren lit a cigarette to take his mind off the throbbing hard-on and let Jon compose himself.

Darren You're not used to this, are you?

Jon   *(he was rumbled)* No.

Darren   You're just nervous, it happens.

Jon put his dick back in his jeans and sat down on the bed. He felt as though he needed to explain things but didn't really know how to begin. So he sighed.

Darren   What's up?

Jon   This! Me! I don't know.

Darren   Do you want to talk about it?

Why do people have to be so nice about it? It doesn't make it any easier for the person afflicted.

Jon   How do you know when you're gay? I mean, what makes you so sure that you are?

Darren   Why – aren't *you* sure?

Jon   I thought I was.

Darren   And how long have you been thinking about it?

Jon   A few days.

Nobody in The Village has time for a fuck-up!

Darren   Then maybe you should think about it some more.

Darren hands Jon his shirt.

Jon   *(almost desperately)* But this is what I want.

Darren   *(bemused)* You can't just want to be gay – you either are or you aren't.

Jon   But how do you know?

Darren   *(bluntly)* You fancy men!

Jon was silent.

Darren   Look. Find yourself a nice girl and forget about it. Being gay isn't just about fuckin' clubs and Canal Street. It's not even about sex.

Jon looked at him – the question on his face.

Darren   It's about who you are inside. Anybody can fuck about, if they want – it doesn't mean they're gay. Being gay's about *who* you fancy, who you *want* to fuck, who you *want* to have a relationship with. And most important of all – who you end up loving. And if it's a bloke, then you're gay! And if it's a woman, then you're unfortunate! But you can't make yourself something you're not. You can't just wake up one morning and want to be gay. It doesn't work like that.

Jon thought for a while and then spoke his heart out…

Jon   Then I am – but am not! *(he laughed to himself)* I'm fucked! *(he heaved a heavy sigh)* I'm so fuckin' fucked!

Now it was Darren's turn to look at Jon with a question on his face.

Jon   Well I can't fuckin' do it, can I!

It was David he wanted – not just anyone.

Chapter Two - Growth

11.39 p.m.   Saturday, 12th July 2003.

There was a knock at Carol's door.

Carol   *(opening the door)* David?

David   I need to talk to you.

She looked into the street. She could feel the draft from the net curtains twitching in the avenue.

Carol   *(as if in fear of being overheard)* I can't.

David   *(exasperated)* Why?

Carol   David. We agreed.

She wanted to shut the door on him and hide.

David   I won't go until you talk to me.

He seemed adamant.

She could almost hear the breeze being generated from the twitching nets of her neighbours.

Carol   *(trying not to appear angry at him)* Don't make this any worse than it already is.

David   I love you!

Her heart was melting. But…

Carol   Go home.

She tried shutting the door, but he wouldn't let her.

David   Then tell me you don't feel the same way. Tell me you don't love me and I'll go – and I'll never come back. Tell me! Tell me you don't love me.

He was getting louder and Carol was getting more nervous.

Carol   You know I can't.

David   *(with tears in his eyes)* So why are you doing this to me?

Carol   I have no choice.

David   Why? *(calmly)* Is there someone else?

Carol   No! No, of course not.

David   So why?

Carol   I have responsibilities. Things you don't know about.

David   So explain to me – make me understand, because right now none of this makes any sense.

Carol   Come in.

They went into the living room and the conversation continued.

Carol   I can't be with you, David, because there is some else.

David's face fell.

Carol My son...

David *(confused)* In Australia?

Carol No, he isn't in Australia. He lives here, with me.

He tried to understand what he'd just been told.

Carol He's a quadriplegic.

David was knocked for six (and then a few other numbers as well).

David What!??

He tried to get his head around it. Why hadn't she mentioned this before?

Carol A quadriplegic.

David I heard what you said. *(bewildered)* Why didn't you tell me?

Carol *(guiltily)* I don't know.

She couldn't look at him. It was all over.

David Didn't you think I'd understand?

He didn't know if he was angry. He really didn't know what to think.

Carol It's not like that. When we first met. *(she tried to look at him)* I didn't want to be known *(but she couldn't)* as just the woman with the disabled son. I wanted to be seen as me, just me. *(tears began to grow in her eyes)* And I'm sorry I lied, I really am, but this is me. The woman with the cripple. *(she turned to look at his response)* So now you know.

She waited, expecting him to say something. Expecting him to leave.

David   It doesn't matter.

Carol   Oh no? You don't feed him, wash him, change his bloody underwear. It matters.

David   Not to me.

Carol   No! But it does to me. I can't do this.

She turns away from him.

David   *(angry that he's not being taken seriously)* So that's it? We're suddenly over just because you've got to look after your son?

Carol   *(almost hysterical)* Yes! Yes! And whether I like it or not that's the way it is – I don't have a choice. So just go! *(apologetic)* It's not your problem.

***

It was 2.30ish on Sunday morning in Essential.

Jon was walking around the building intent on seeing David. But with three floors of wall-to-wall human debris it was hard to see wheat from chaff.

Like the night before, the atmosphere was heavy and dark. Bodies moved in and out of his vision. Some smiled, some leered, some could hardly focus, smacked off their tits on a cocktail of Pils and pills. And then he saw him…

Jon   *(shouting)* David!

But you could hardly hear your own voice above the constant beat of the music. So David lead him out of a fire door into the stairwell.

David   *(he was not happy)* What?

Jon   I'm sorry about the other night.

He waited for David to accept the apology and say it was 'OK' – but he didn't.

Jon   Look, I was drunk. I didn't know what I was saying.

David   You seem to be making a habit out of this.

Jon was fucking it up again!

Jon   Please, I want to explain.

David didn't see the point, but allowed Jonathan his moment.

Jon   *(he gave a deep sigh before he began)* It's hard, you know. This, with you, I don't know what am feeling half the time. But the other night, when I saw you with that guy, I knew then.

David   You knew what?

Jon   *(he smiled)* Do I have to say it?

This just pissed him off.

David   I can do without this.

He turned to leave. Jonathan had jerked him around enough already.

Jon   David?

David   *(with great venom)* Look! Just leave it, alright!

Jon   But this is what I want.

David	*(still with venom)* What *you* want? What you fuckin' want? What about what I want? What about me?
Jon	*(taken aback)* I thought…
David	…You thought, did you? Well you 'thought' wrong.

Jonathan was confused. And as he tried to work it out David had started to head-off up the stairs to The Pop Lounge.

Jon	Wait!

David stopped and turned. He gave him another two barrels!

David	No! You wait! You can't fuck people around like this. One minute you're gay and then next you don't wanna know. Well, fuck you! Fuck you!
Jon	*(pleading)* I didn't know what I was doing. I didn't know what I was.
David	So you usually shag blokes on a night out do you?
Jon	What?
David	The night you stopped over…

Jonathan just looked at him vacantly.

>…Fuck you!

He carried on walking, and Jonathan followed.

Jon	I don't know what you mean.

David   Look! If you're straight, you're straight. Fine! Good luck to you. Just fuck off back to Deansgate[141] and leave us all in peace.

He just wanted to get through the door at the top of the stairs and away from Jonathan.

Jon   It's not like that! I wasn't fucking you about. I didn't even know that had happened... With the K and all that...!

David   *(he didn't believe him)* Really?!?

How could you have sex with a guy and not know?

Jon   Really, I didn't know what I was doing that night.

And that was genuine. He'd thought it was a dream. A fantasy. The drugs.

Jon   It was the first time anything like that had ever happened to me. I was confused. I didn't know what I wanted. I wasn't gay, or at least I didn't think I was. And then the other night, when I saw you with that guy, I knew.

David   You were jealous.

And for the first time the penny dropped. In fact, you could hear it rolling down the stairwell. Jon only wanted him back because he'd seen him with somebody else.

Jon   Ye'.

David   So what do you want me to do about it?

---

[141] An area in Manchester that gay people see as synonymous with heterosexual nights out.

Jon   *(his voice showed his despair)* I don't know.

It was almost a whine, that just made David angry.

David   You must have some idea. You're here, aren't you?

Jon   I wanted to see you.

It sounded pathetic even to Jonathan.

David   And now you are.

There was no answer from Jon, so David just shrugged at him and started to walk away.

Jon   *(after him)* I didn't mean for any of this to happen. It's just that it did, and I'm sorry. I'm not trying to fuck you about. I don't know how I'm feeling half the time. You don't know what it's like.

David just looked at him.

David   *(angrily)* Really? You think I wasn't confused when I first came out? You think you're the only one who's ever gone through all this?

Jonathan didn't know what to say. It wasn't because he was jealous… In his heart he knew he wanted David – not because David was gay, but because he was him!

The more Jon thought about who and what he was, the more he realised his 'queer' streak had boundaries. It's like when you're straight, you don't fancy every girl you see – in fact, some girls are pretty repulsive. It's the same with guys, and with Jonathan it was most guys. That's why he couldn't do it with Darren – it's because he wasn't gay!

In fact, Jonathan only fancied one guy – and that was David. And him being a guy was immaterial. He could have been a girl or a goat, it wouldn't have mattered – this was about who he was, not what he was.

Jon   I'm sorry. I don't know what else to say. Please? Just give me another chance.

David thought for a while and without saying a word offered Jon his hand. And with that they entered the belly of the beast and joined the party.

Two E's – and an hour later – they were living the moment once again. The moment when they first met. Locked into one another, they danced and moved with the crowed around them. Neither of them seeing it – neither of them knowing it – their total attention fixed, one upon the other. And as the hours rolled by, the night became morning and the dark became light – and the day began with them, emerging from the club, as lovers.

***

At David's flat, woozy on ketamine, they kissed. A slow, passionate, full-on, sensual kiss, the type you see in movies, the type that gives you a hard-on if you watch it – and pre-cum[142] if you receive it. It was a moment time remembers. With the music from the club still beating in their heads – like a movie soundtrack[143] – it filled the silence. And, if this was being gay, thought Jonathan, then he was

---

[142] Pre-cum is a clear, sticky liquid produced by the erect penis prier to the ejaculation of semen – biologically produced as a lubricant to assist penetration during intercourse.
[143] Flip & Fill's *Shooting Star (2001)*.

glad. And if it wasn't, then he was still glad. This was a moment in time he would never forget. And it just kept on getting better.

***

Under the influence of drugs our bodies melted into one another and their sex seemed seamless... Endless - sensual - gliding - sliding - soft - like a sea of me - and him - limb softened limb. In - blending - bending - doubling - lending - time standing still - filling -emptying - adding - reversing - never subtracting. Moving forward - into and onto - beyond and back. Here and now - sharing his skin - in to him - in him - below his surface - borrowing his outer shell... Sweating - sliding and gliding on white sheets - like soft pasta shells drizzled with oil - glistening in the half-light...Underneath his form - warm - sweat lubricating - passion... Ekstasis! Religion is the here - near - no fear of damnation now. This is love - and death.

If Jonathan died right now...

And amidst it all Jonathan came to realise.

It's true what they say about men – they do give better blow jobs than women.

And, instinctively, he too could give good head!

***

When Jonathan was with him, he felt like he was being himself. With girls he'd always had to 'make an effort' and try. It didn't mean that he didn't make an effort when he was with David, but it was different – he didn't have to try. He didn't have to pretend. When he was with a girl, he felt like he had to play a part, like he was acting all the time, thinking about everything he had to do to try to impress her, but with him he just knew how to be. He just knew. With him it was just total. Before he met David, satisfaction came from what he did to girls. Now it came from what they did together, what David did to him. Sex with was fun with David – a total experience, not just a physical action of 'doing it' anymore.

***

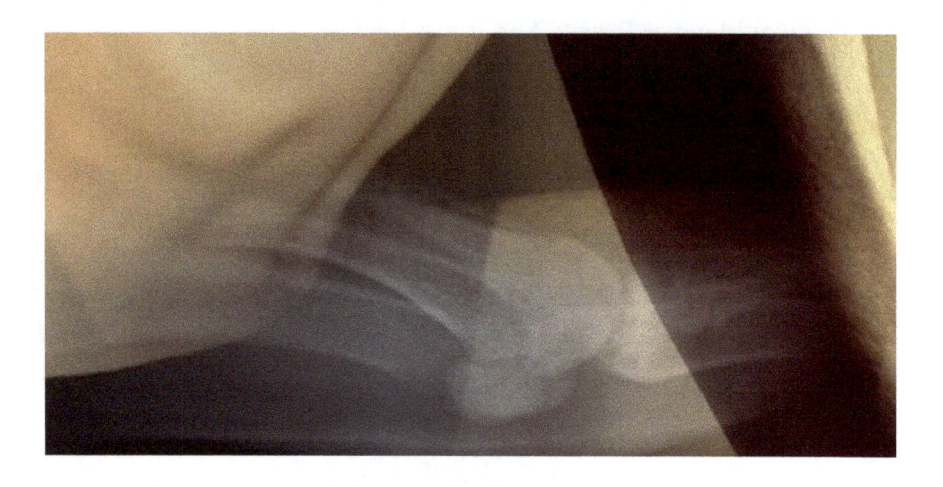

Sleep hit them around 9.00 a.m.,[144] as they passed out in one another's arms. The two naked bodies peacefully entwined, like a Michelangelo. If you ever believed that homosexuality was an ugly thing, they would have proved you wrong. They lay there, in heaven. Like two angels embraced in slumber. One dark, one fair. The beautiful innocence of their bodies, muscular and feminine; heroic and classical. It was as though God himself had sculpted them, just to prove how sexy two boys could be.

***

That night was like coming home. It was like I'd been missing him all my life; like feeling homesick for somewhere I'd never been.

***

Like a shadow - our inner-self is always there, waiting to be illuminated... It's in our deepest, darkest desires and fears. Acknowledge the shadow in yourself - *own your shadow*! Too many people deny it - try to lock it away, but at night - as they sleep - it walks abroad in their dreams. To deny it - to not acknowledge its

---

[144] After two hours of full-on foreplay.

existence causes it to eats away at you - like a child that's denied it's parent's love, it will turn against you - frustrated at not being allowed its independence - and by suppressing it - a time-bomb - waiting to blow. The uncontrolled release of an angry desire - it can do something stupid - and manifest itself in serial killers, paedophiles, rapists and stalkers.

In our dreams we all walk alone. Our uniqueness is inside - the outer-self is for others. The social grooming and the thin veneer of civilisation is all just an illusion. As we bite our tongues to stop us saying something, we fight with ourselves to stop us acting on the impulses we all feel, but are too ashamed to acknowledge.

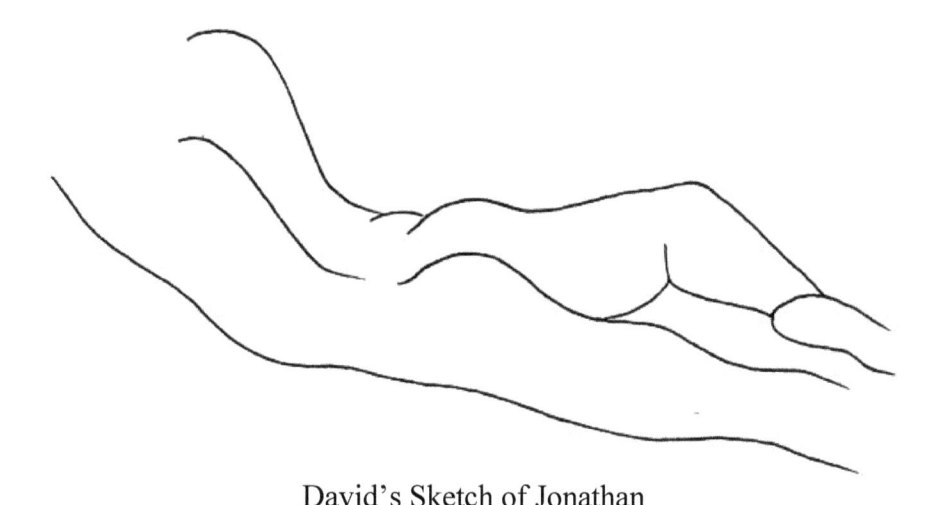

David's Sketch of Jonathan

Chapter Three - Movement

M

8.30 p.m.   Sunday, 13th July 2003.

There was a knock at the door. It was David.

Carol   I didn't think I'd see you again.

But she was glad she did.

David   Then you don't know me very well.

Carol led him through into the lounge.

Carol   Tea?

David   In a minute.

He kissed her tenderly on the lips.

The kiss was soft and gentle. She didn't resist, and so he kissed her again. This time his lips parting. Her's parting to. He placed his arms around her and then…

Carol   I can't.

It was all getting too serious.

>   What about him?

This was her defence for everything.

David	I don't care. I want you.
Carol	Not here. Not like this.
David	Then where? You name it. My place, where ever!
Carol	I can't just do things like that.
David	Why?
Carol	Because…
David	…Because of him?

Gesturing upstairs.

Carol	Yes. Yes! Because of him!

Their voices were becoming raised and Carol fell silent. David knew he'd pushed her too far and felt guilty.

David	*(with sympathy)* It doesn't have to be like this.
Carol	You're such a sweet boy.

She raised her hand and softly caressed his cheek. In her heart she felt the future drain away – but as she looked into his clear blue eyes.

David	Come upstairs with me.
Carol	*(a nervous giggle in her voice)* What?
David	Come upstairs…
Carol	*(still with a nervous giggle)* I don't think so.
David	Frightened?
Carol	No! *(pause)* Maybe.

David   I love you, Carol. And I want to show you how much.

They made love like they do in novels. Classy novels. Novels that ladies read – written by other ladies a long time ago, in an age when romance was more important than rude words, and fucking hadn't been invented.

It was a different world, with different values.

And different people.

***

Sex had been gentle and loving. She'd felt safe, wanted, loved, and as she lay in his arms, she caught sight of herself in the dressing table mirror. This sagging old woman in the arms of a young god and she felt ashamed, guilty, dirty even.

She quickly grabbed up her dressing gown and covered herself.

Carol   I need the toilet.

She locked the bathroom door behind her and cried. She cried out all the shame she could find. The beauty of him made it even worse. Her own body creased and tattered was made more so by his perfection. She could never be with him. And the way she felt was this: he, with whom she had never felt so loved, now made her feel so old, he, with whom she had never felt so safe, now made her feel so insecure, he, with whom she had never felt so wanted, now made her feel uglier than she had ever felt in her whole life. But she knew that it wasn't him that made her feel this way – it was herself.

>   She can't bear him touching her
>   and she hungered for it
>   and now it starves her
>   and the thought of it...
>   feeding her
>   and the nature of what they have done
>   making her wretch
>   and how she has craved
>   and how...
>   and how...
>   and she still wants...
>   and she still needs...
>   the hunger is still there

There was a gentle knock at the door and then a whisper.

David   Are you OK?

Carol   *(sniffing back the tears)* I'm fine.

David   Would you like a cup of tea?

Carol   I'll make it in a minute.

David   I'll make it!

She heard him head down the stairs and she cried again. This time for his beautiful heart. Beauty should only lie with beauty. And swine should only ever drink swill. She opened her robe and looked at herself in the mirror. Her body was a map of her life. Every line and crease. Every roll of fat and flesh she knew like a well-read story. Her story. The story of birth and death. Of years and tears, and Christmases gone, where she'd eaten too much and exercised too little. And him, he was a story yet to be written. A tale yet to be told. How could they…

She closed her eyes and then the robe. It offended her more than she could bear to see.

David   Tea?

She opened the door and was greeted with a smile. He was dressed in only his boxer shorts. His golden hair tussled. His stomach and chest rippling with youthful muscle. She felt sick.

David   Are you sure you're OK?

Carol just smiled a fake smile and nodded.

David   What is it?

Carol   Nothing. Honestly.

It was as sincere as she could make it. And pulled her dressing gown tightly around her.

David   Is it me? Have I done something wrong?

Carol   *(shocked he could ever think such a thing)* No! God no!

She realised how her disgust must have been misread.

Carol   It's me. It's not you. I should never have done this. It wasn't right.

David   *(pleading)* Why?

Carol   I'm old enough to be your mother.

David looked at her but said nothing.

Carol   And you're young enough to be my son.

David   It doesn't matter. Not if we love one another.

Carol   It does. To me it matters.

David   Because of what people might say?

Carol   No. Because of how I feel.

It was obvious he didn't understand. She would have to explain.

Carol   You are such a beautiful young man. Beautiful! And I feel... well... I should get dressed.

It was an excuse to stop looking at him.

David   It's being here, isn't it?

He was no psychiatrist but he was sure the surroundings couldn't be conducive to relaxed night of passion.

David   We could go back to mine. Get on the next bus out of here – 'leave the world behind and start a new someplace else'.

Even he didn't know why he'd started talking like a character from *Gone with the Wind*[145]

Carol   But what about him?

David   Just leave him.

Carol   I couldn't do that.

David   You can do anything – if you really want to.

Carol   Then maybe I just don't want to enough.

David   Maybe you're just frightened.

---

[145] *Gone with the Wind* – a movie made in 1939, by director David O. Selznick, starring Clark Gable, as Rhett Butler, and Vivien Leigh, as Scarlett O'Hara, based on the romantic novel by Margaret Mitchell, set during the American Civil War of 1861–65.

Carol   You're asking me to leave everything behind. Everything I know. I don't know if I can do that.

David   Do you want to?

Carol   Want doesn't come into it.

David   Then what does?

Carol   It wouldn't be right. People like me don't run away. We can't!

David   And what are 'People like you?'

Carol   I don't know.

David   I want to make love to you, Carol. I want to take you in my arms and make love to you under the stars.

Carol looked into his eyes and then he kissed her. She was being kissed by God in his boxers and all she could think about was the state of her hair.

**

Maybe a fantasy is only ever truly real when it remains just that – a fantasy.

And in the light of day she'd realised that she was no Scarlet O'Hara, even if he couldn't give a damn!

Sketch by David

Chapter Four - Self

3.13 p.m.   Monday, 14th July 2003.

In the garden with Enid, Carol and The Spastic... Like a really shit daytime chat show you would find on Channel Five or one of those free Sky channels no one watches.

Enid   I see your roses are out.

Carol loved nature, despite what it had done to her.

They're not the only things 'Out'!

Carol   I know, I've been lucky this year. The dahlias are nice as well.

This was banal even by their standards. Had they run out of things to talk about? Or were there just so many things, they didn't know how to start?

Enid   Seen any more of your bus stop boy?

Jonathan's ears pricked up, as he hurtled from his day-dream back to reality.

Carol   *(with an embarrassed girly tone)* Give over!

But Enid could read it. They'd been friends for far too long for either of them to hide anything from the other.

Enid   You have, haven't you?

What was she suggesting?

Carol   No.

Enid   Carol?

Even thought she was bursting to tell her. She knew she never could, or would.

Carol   He looks over the hedge every once in a while, that's all.

She was playing it cool.

Enid   Just enough to give you a flush, aye?

If only she knew.

Carol   Stop it. He's a very nice lad, and nothing more.

She wanted to change the subject before she said too much.

Enid   What's his name then?

Carol   David.

The way she said it spoke volumes. Jonathan couldn't miss the sigh in his name.

Enid   You've done your homework then?

She'd done more than that.

Carol   *(with a smile)* He lives at number 23 and he studies Art at the University.

Enid   Asked to see his etchings yet?

Carol laughed.

Carol   No I haven't, and I'm not going to neither.

Enid   Mind if I do then? It would be a shame to let him go to waste. I've always fancied being done in oils.

Enid was a mucky bitch when she got a few gins down her and today she'd had more than a few.

Carol   Ooo, you are a one.

Enid   So, what else is new?

And the subject was over, and Jonathan drifted back into his own world.

***

David's flat.

Charlie   So is he, or isn't he?

David   He is when he's with me.

Charlie   I'll take that as a 'yes' then.

They drank tea and smiled at one another.

Charlie   I presume you're seeing him again?

David   *(nonchalantly)* I might.

Charlie   'I might'. How fuckin' begging for it are you?

She said launching a playful cushion as David's head.

David   I'm not 'begging for it'.

She gave him a 'pull the other one' look out of the corner of her eye.

David   He's as full-on about this as I am.

Charlie   *(with a little disbelief)* Really?

David   Really.

Charlie (*in a patronising tone*) Then I hope you'll both be very happy. When's the wedding?

David threw back the cushion.

David (*jokingly*) Fuck off!

Charlie Well, I need to know. I want to buy a big 'fuck-off' hat!

David What? For your big 'fuck-off' head!

They fell into fits of giggles. The cushion being introduced, once again, as a missile.

Charlie (*giggling uncontrollably*) Stop! Stop! I'll wet myself.

David Eeerrr! Get off the bed you pissy bitch!

They both landed on the floor laughing. Laying there, side-by-side, staring up at the shitty papered ceiling, like an ABBA album cover.

Charlie (*serious*) Don't let him fuck you about.

After the laughter and histrionics this seemed even more solemn.

David I won't. (*in his defence*) He's got problems. (*qualifying himself*) He's just coming out, we all make mistakes when that happens.

Charlie I just don't want you to get hurt again, that's all.

David I know.

He tilted his head and gave Charlie a delicate 'sisterly' kiss on the cheek.

Charlie (*sensing a moment*) You out tonight?

She broke the atmosphere with a change of subject.

David   Monday night? Cruz? Do I look desperate? Don't answer that! *(with a joke smugness)* Anyhow, you forget – I have a boyfriend now!

Charlie   *(singing the taunt)* 'You got a boyfriend, you wanna love him, you wanna kiss him, you wanna marry him…'

David   *(joking)* Fuck off!

He thwacks her with the cushion.

Charlie   *(in giggly pain)* Aaaww!

David   Serves you right!

Charlie   That was the zip!

Rubbing the side of her head.

David   You were lucky it wasn't the candlestick![146]

Charlie   Fuckin' Mrs Plumb![147]

David   Fuckin' Miss Piss!

As always, their conversation dissolved into childish insult, with a modicum of playful violence.

---

[146] An illusion to the whodunit board game Cluedo. Of which, one of the murder weapons is a candlestick.

[147] Mrs Plumb is not, however, a character in the game Cluedo. But sounds like she should be!

Chapter Five - Flow

1.46 p.m.   Tuesday, 15th July 2003.

Carol paces the living room. She picks up a cushion; she wasn't sure whether she was trying to plump it or kill it. She was waiting for David. There was a knock at the door. It was him. The cushion heaved a sigh of relief!

David   *(concerned)* I came round as soon as I could. What is it?

Carol   *(panic in her voice)* Sit down.

This felt ominous.

Carol   I've decided.

David   What?

He feared the worse.

Carol   I do want to be with you.

The smile on David's face grew as the fear subsided.

David   *(his face beaming)* What made you change your mind?

He stood up to face her.

Carol   You did. Life's too short to waste like this.

Her voice still held grave doubts about what she was doing.

David   And what about Jonathan?

The concern was genuine.

Carol   He'll be better off in a Home. They'll take care of him there.

She said the words, but they were cold.

David   You're sure about this?

Carol   No.

The ice broke and tears trickled down her face. *Why is life so fucking difficult?*

David   You're making the right decision, I promise you.

He kissed her.

I hope so.

***

The first man Carol slept with was the man she married, and their first night together was their wedding night. He was her first and her only, and she was his. And the fear of it all, she remembers shaking. They did. In those days, you met a boy, you 'courted', got engaged, got married, had children and that's what happened. It's what was expected of you, and that was it – there was nothing else.

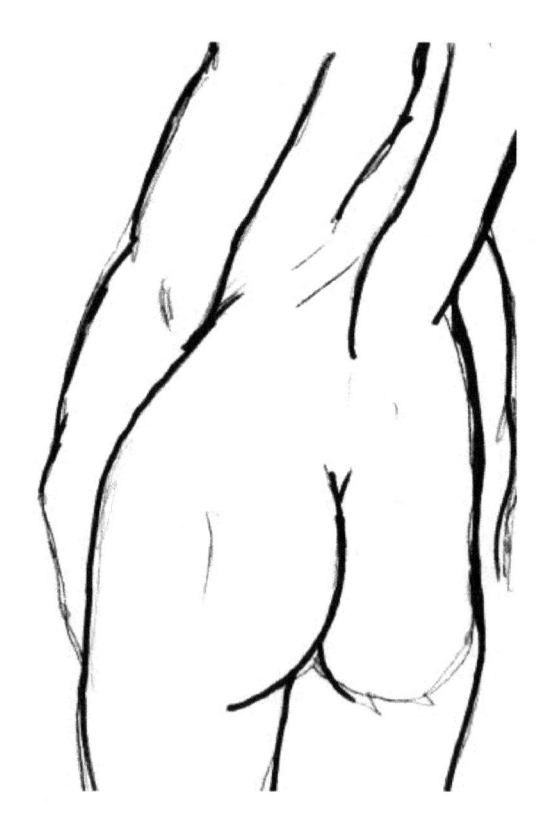

You ask, did she love him? Yes... Yes, she did. He was the father of her child. And she was happy. She didn't want for anything more than that. She didn't need anymore than that. Dreams and aspirations were different then. Not better, not worse, just different. Bob was a good man – a good father. In those days you didn't marry for passion, you married a decent, hardworking, man who treated you well. And by the end she did love him. You see, there comes a time in your life when you have to settle for what you can have, not necessarily what you want. There comes a time when you realise: this is as good as it gets, and you can dream all you want but the clock is ticking – you can feel it – and you take what you're offered.

***

She never noticed the sixties. It happened somewhere else for her – it didn't happen there. The world was grey in those days – like the films they show on the telly. It was after the war, and it felt as though, if you had fun it was wrong, because people had died and the living felt guilty. It was all antimacassars[148] and durable furniture

---

[148] Antimacassars were the clothes they put on the arms and backs of chairs to stop them from being soiled.

– all heavy and dark. It was a time when even the children looked serious, like little adults – the boys with their Brylcreemed hair[149] and suits, the girls, with their hair all set ready for the dance in the church hall. Carol had felt, all her life, like she'd been middle aged - responsible, respectable, frightened. That fear... Her values and morals were from a different world - a world that didn't exist anymore. And you wake up one day and you're living in a time warp. It's not just the clothes that have changed - it's the way you live - the way you think...

Suburbia – a ghetto for people waiting to die – who then go to heaven and spend an eternity in chintz.

To have that time over again, would she have done things any different?

I think so... It was like I always lived in fear. The fear of the repercussions, of what people might say or do. It's like I've been playing someone else all my life. First, I was the daughter, then the shop girl, the wife, the mother. The one person I never played in all that was me. I never really played me. And now? Being yourself is frightening. Having to think about what you want out of life. Having to live it for yourself and not through other people. That's frightening.

***

In the end you just close your mind...

***

Part of this doesn't feel like me. I'm doing something that I'm not brought up to deal with – something that only happens to other people.

***

---

[149] Brylcreem was the trademark name of a brilliantine hair product, used for flattening and smoothing hair since the 19th century.

When he's not here I miss him. I miss him all the time. He's on my mind. I catch myself just picturing him. Replaying the times when we're together. He fills my day and when I kiss him, his lips are soft. Things like this don't happen to me. It's like I'm watching someone else – like I'm being someone else – and it feels like I'm acting in a film. And deep down inside I'm saying, 'This isn't me... This isn't me...' And I wish someone would walk in on us and see me.

***

Mother   Ready for your dinner? What are you looking at then? Are you watching the children play? That's nice.

She can hardly look at him – she feels so ashamed of herself.

Outside the window two boys were playing in the street, their strong playful knocks, their rough and tumble. Jonathan's unnoticed eye noticed it all. Spying on their private world, as one boy lost and never found, he remembers a friend he once had.

***

Jonathan – when he was *'Jonny'* – had lots of friends. His best friend was Andy; they went to the same junior school, the same secondary school... They probably would have gone into the same sixth form together, if things had been different. When someone's always been around, you get used to them being there. Whether you want it or not, you end up behaving like a married couple. Jonny and Andy were no exception...

They would go to Andy's house after school, and they would hit the house like a whirlwind. At thirteen you do everything like the Tasmanian Devil,[150] from opening doors to taking your coat off; the

---

[150] A cartoon character that destroys everything he touches and is always pictured (when moving) as a cyclone.

simplest of jobs, like 'taking a shower', become a sequence from a Jackie Chan movie.[151] And, as always, they had their routines.

Andy raided the fridge, for drinks – he grabs two cans (*Tizer* and *Coke*) and hands Jonny his favourite... *Tizer*!

Jonny   Cheers!

They bound up-stairs to the privacy of Andy's lair... As tradition has it, they kick off their shoes, rip off their blazers and immerse themselves in *Streetfighter* on the Super Nintendo... This will continue until one of three things happens: 1) They get hungry, 2) They need the toilet, or 3) A parent intervenes. In *Streetfighter* the aim of the game is to beat-up your opponent – and that's why it's called a 'beat-em-up' game. Jonny is always Ryu and Andy is always Ken.[152] Like any adolescent male, anywhere in the world, they communicate through basic sounds rather than language.[153] Conversation takes up too much thought and isn't necessary for the playing of *Streetfighter*.

And there they would sit, on Andy's bed, bobbing and swearing, umbilically linked to the TV screen, like a little married couple, feeling every action of their virtual world in unison.

This was their young life together. Girls happened, and didn't happen, around this central relationship. There was no doubt which came first. There was no question as to what – or *who* – was more important to them.

After the accident Andy went round to see him. At first it was every day. Then once a week. Then months would pass by, and, before he knew it, he'd stopped calling round. Jonny disappeared and Jonathan took his place.

---

[151] Jackie Chan is Chinese actor who specialises in fast-moving fight sequences and action movies, such as *The One* and *Shanghai Noon*.
[152] The characters are an even match, with the same sort of moves. Only Ken's a little more impatient and aggressive... How can you tell from a computer game? When you play them every waking moment you can just tell.
[153] Why talk when you can grunt?

***

I wonder what he's doing right now?

***

Andy worked for a call centre. He worked 12 'til 9, Monday to Friday. He travelled to work on the tram. He had nights out in Deansgate. Went clubbing every fortnight and had a curry, from Rusholme, once a week, and every now and again he'd think of 'Jonny'.

I wonder how he is?

He'd make himself promises to go round and see him – but that was six years ago.

He probably won't even remember me now.

And that excused him… But Jonathan did remember him – for a long time it's all he could do: 'Remember'.

Nothing lasts forever.

Chapter Six - People

9.53 a.m.	Wednesday, 16th July 2003.

Another day. Another normality.

Mother	Sun's out again.

She tried to keep it that way. Her secret burning inside her. Every word she checked to make sure it didn't come out as: 'I'm putting you in a Home'.

Mother	Do you want to go out in the garden again? Want to see the birdies?

No, I want to see David.

Mother	Open wide.

He takes the food.

Mother	Is it nice?

But he's thinking about David.

Mother	Oh, we're spilling. All over that nice clean shirt. We are a mucky pup!

Maybe she can read my mind.

But for once she didn't care.

***

David's flat.

It was late afternoon. David and Jon had just fucked, and the room was hot and smelt of sex. They lay on the bed together. The covers thrown back to allow their bodies to breathe. It was one of those moments that only students have.[154]

Jon   I'm hot.

There was a really cheesy joke there, but David didn't take it.

David   I'll get you some water.

He was about to get up when Jon stopped him.

Jon   No, don't go. Let's just lie here.

David put his arm around Jon and rested his head on his chest.

David   Are you happy?

Jon   *(dreamily)* Blissfully. And you?

David   *(smiling)* Ye'.

They lay in silence for a while before David spoke again.

David   So, what finally made up your mind?

Jon   I don't know, it was a feeling, I just had to.

And as he searched for the right words to use, he seemed to get more and more lost in what it was he wanted to say.

---

[154] As well as French Expressionist painters from Paris, circa 1920.

David	I knew I was gay when I was a kid. Used to fancy people on the telly all the time. Do you remember *Power Rangers*?[155]
Jon	*(a curious laughing)* Ye'!
David	I fancied the red one – Jason.

Jon half laughed at the idea that someone could feel sexual desire for a cartoon character – and then remembered his own experience.

Jon	I was more into Chun-Li.[156]
David	So when did you first start fancying lads?
Jon	When I met you.

The genuine answer was a conversation killer. It wasn't a corny line, or an ounce of flattery. It was the truth. And it sat there, as the truth does, until he spoke again.

Jon	That's what did my head in. I was just normal till I met you.

That word 'normal' jarred.

David	And now you don't think you're normal?
Jon	I didn't mean it to sound like that.
David	But you think it?
Jon	Maybe?

---

[155] *The Mighty Morphin Power Rangers* was a Saturday morning children's TV show from Japan, which began screening in the UK in 1993. It featured five teenagers who 'morphed' into Power Rangers to defend the earth from the powers of darkness – transforming themselves 'collectively' into a Megazord.

[156] The female fight character from the *Streetfighter* computer game.

David sat up.

David   We're as normal as anyone else…

Jon   But we're not, are we? Two lads sleeping together… It isn't normal.

David was sleeping with a homophobe.[157] He felt his back stiffen as he comprehended the scenario. He was still straight, after all.

David   Maybe this was a bad idea.

The mood in the flat changed and David was feeling uncomfortable. He started to get up.

Jon   *(trying to get him to stay in bed)* David?

But he just wanted to get up and put his clothes on. Maybe he would feel more comfortable then?

David   Let's just leave it, aye?

Jon   What's that supposed to mean?

David   I can't do this.

Jon   'Do' what?

David   When I came 'Out' I did it because I wasn't going to live like this! I wasn't going to be made to feel like this.

Jon   Like what? Explain to me?

David   This!

---

[157] Homophobe – someone who has a fear or hatred of gay people.

Words had ceased to work anymore. David couldn't express what 'this' was anymore than Jon could understand it. 'This' was more than a situation, it was a whole state of mind. The whole meaning of life, David's life!

***

One day a gay man wakes up and decided he's going to play a game of Russian Roulette. He takes a gun (with six chambers), loads a single bullet into one of the chambers, points the gun at his head and pulls the trigger. If he's lucky he only has to do this once. This is coming out!

For David, 'coming out' was about being accepted for who and what he was. To keep his sexuality a secret was to deny who he was; in his eyes, it would also feel as though he'd accepted that what he did was wrong, that it needed to be hidden as some sordid, dirty little secret. He wasn't going to do that, and that's why he picked up the gun.

When you gamble your friends and family – everyone you've every known and cared about – on a confession[158] that could destroy your whole world (and theirs with it) you never see things through the same eyes ever again. And they never see you through the same eyes either.[159]

Jon made David feel dirty! It was as though he was calling him a queer for sleeping with a man, even though he was the man he'd slept with. I know it doesn't make sense, but David didn't want to sleep with someone who felt guilty about it, and that's what he felt Jon was feeling – guilty about having sex with a man.

The truth of the matter was, Jon didn't feel guilty at all. He felt free and liberated. The concept of what 'normal' meant to Jon was

---

[158] That single silver bullet of honesty.

[159] And it's not as though you chose this for yourself. How many people have to 'come out' as being disabled or ginger? How many people lose their families because they confess to being black? Do straight people have to admit their sexual preferences to their parents? 'Mum, I've got something to tell you. I'm into *autoerotic asphyxiation*.' It doesn't happen to them – they don't have to go through a sexual confession.

different. 'Normal' was something he wanted to escape from - it was restrictive, suppressive, controlling, unfulfilling, mediocre, with David he had found someone he could be himself with, and it didn't matter that he was a man. For Jonathan not being 'normal' was positive not negative.

***

David got dressed, so did Jonathan. They didn't speak.

Words had failed them.

***

A Quick Lesson in Sexual Politics

In our 'physical' world we have 'things' that are 'material'. Things we can touch, and hold, and own. Having 'material things' in this world seems to prove that we exist; wealth and property bind us into this reality – they bind us to the earth.

Lack of freedom, a mortgage, financial restraints. We become 'wage slaves'. We become trapped - crippled - disabled. In the days of Slave Trading - to stop slaves from running away from their owners they were 'hobbled'.[160] Birds have their wings clipped to stop them from flying away - to hold them to the ground - to deny their freedom and flight. Ownership is about tying things down - grasping - holding on to things. We store - lock up - put away - hoard our possessions, and so we bind to us that which we hold most dear.[161]

Take the idea of marriage, a cultural concept that, traditionally, makes a wife 'property' of her husband.[162] Marriage was never natural. Marriage

---

[160] This was the process of cutting their ankle tendons to literally 'stop them from being able to run'.
[161] Dear – a term of affection, and a term for an expensive price tag!
[162] Originally marriage was designed to bind females and males together; for the male, it ensured that his mate's offspring were genetically his, by making her exclusive to him, and for the female, it ensured that she would be fed and protected

was a way of 'binding' people together for survival in a world that hasn't existed for thousands of years. Surveys show that between 54% and 75% of couples – irrespective of the bonding traditions in different countries or their social frameworks – cheat on their partners while professing to be in a monogamous relationship. The general consensus is that many marriages fail because human males aren't programmed to be monogamous.[163] Our primal emotions drive men to want to impregnate as many females as possible with their genetic make up. The more babies he can make the more chances he has of having one child surviving to adulthood. Babies are fragile, they are vulnerable, and they die. Science doesn't let this happen anymore[164] – most babies live – but our primitive instinct isn't capable of adapting to that. Man, with his mind, has developed a world in advance of his emotional ability to cope with it.

So marriage was 'developed' to make sure our species didn't die out. Religion originally used ceremonies to mark the event, publicly announcing the exclusivity of a union to others in the community.[165] Organised Religion hijacked the ceremonies to emotionally bind the union, and the resulting offspring, into a contract with the Church.[166] As The Church was able to control its followers with 'the fear of god' - community leaders could ally themselves with religion and use their power to control the community. As The Church's power and influence grew within The State, so did its ability to control its followers (and visa versa). Man is trapped!

---

during the pregnancy (which, in comparison to other species, is a long time to be gestating and vulnerable), and the long period of childcare that followed (which is, once again, an amazingly long time for a young animal to be dependent on its parents). With high infant mortality, having children survive was of prime importance to both males and females of the species.

[163] A contention supported in books such as, Christopher Ryan's *Sex at Dawn*, Stephanie Coonz's *The Way We Never Were* and Elisabeth Sheff's *The Polyamorists Next Door*.

[164] And our world has no predators to eat our young, in fact, our environment in the developed world is very safe and extremely child-friendly.

[165] It is at this point 'ownership' becomes evident as Man settles, develops communities and begins farming the land – land and cattle becomes property – civilisation thus becomes a byword for ownership!

[166] The more people you have in your religion the more power it gets, the more power it receives the more power it can have over you.

The Church has always discouraged homosexuality as a sexual practice because it doesn't produce children.[167] If it doesn't produce children then it doesn't strengthen The Church's power base.[168] The other reason behind this 'discouragement' may be even more sinister. Why is it, do you think, The Catholic Church denies its priests the right to marry? Is it so they can concentrate on their spiritual duties? Or is it about The Church being able to subjugate an individual?[169] For any religion to have power it has to be able to control its followers. If you own the bodies and the minds of the people, then you have that power.

The Church and The State together have tamed mankind into submission - mind, body and soul (The Church even mediates with God on our behalf) - so that we can be governed. Marriage, work, home and children are all the things we are groomed to aspire to. All of the things that tie us to responsibility and duty. If we act on our impulses (and refuse to bind ourselves to one partner for life) then we shed our responsibilities. By, not having children, and not having a duty to others (we are outside of the community) we become autonomous and 'we can please ourselves' with what we do.
This is the fear of the homosexual!

Homosexuality, in the Christian Church,[170] is not a sin. The Bible,[171] or any other religious teaching, makes no mention of homosexuality as a perversion – or that it is against the will of any god. Organised Religion hates homosexuality because homosexuality is beyond its control!

---

[167] The same reason why the Catholic Church bans contraception and opposes abortion. Life is only sacred because, once upon a time, we were in short supply. Religion may once have saved us from extinction, now it only serves to control us.
[168] This is also true for The State and explains why many governments have 'outlawed' homosexuality.
[169] And what greater power has anybody than the power to stop one of nature's greatest urges – the power to reproduce!
[170] And within Judaism, Hinduism, Buddhism, Islam and Sikhism.
[171] *See* Appendix XI.

With a world population of over 6,204,850,174[172] the human race is hardly short of offspring – medical science ensures that infant mortality is the lowest in the whole animal kingdom – so Man's duty to reproduce for the species no longer exists. This means that his duty to marry no longer exists. Man now has sex for pleasure, not necessarily for reproduction. This is the interesting bit; if men are biologically programmed to be promiscuous, and women are biologically programmed to develop relationships, then the different sexes share little in common, and would therefore bond better with their own gender group. And if the only reason the two sexes really need to come together is for reproduction – why would you need to fuck someone of the opposite sex if it was just for pleasure? Surely a man knows how to best please a male body, and a woman how to do the same for a female one? If sex is for pleasure alone and not for the conception of children, then it must seem logical that homosexuality is the best and most natural option to achieve this. It also makes more sense in terms of the way we seem to be emotionally programmed.

Homosexuality, as a 'label', has only been around since the 1880s[173]; before that 'homosexual sex' was just something you did or didn't do – it didn't define you like it does now. During the Victorian era[174] we built museums,[175] colonised countries,[176] reformed, sorted, categorised and identified. The British Empire collected and labelled everything it came across,[177] including sexuality. The Empire's Christian morality spanned the globe and tried to homogenise every culture it came into contact with –

---

[172] The UN World Population Counter on 11th February, 2002 at 9.20 am. 30% of whom are under the age of 15. So, there are 4,343,395,122 adults and 1,861,455,052 children.

[173] The word 'homosexual' was created in 1869 by the Hungarian physician Karoly Maria Benkent.

[174] 1837–1901 (Victoria came to the throne at the age of 18).

[175] The Victoria and Albert Museum opened in 1851 and The Natural History Museum opened in South Kensington in 1881.

[176] Colonies and protectorates include: Hong Kong 1841, The Gold Coast 1874, Cyprus 1878, Borneo and Brunei 1880, Egypt 1882, Rhodesia 1889 and Uganda 1894 (Victoria even became Empress of India in 1876).

[177] Charles Darwin published *The Origin of Species* in 1859.

because, let's face it, it's difficult to control something that doesn't respond in a uniform and predictable manner.[178]

Gay men are free to have sex without responsibility and duty. The State and The Church cannot bind them and therefore it cannot control them. What you cannot control becomes frightening. This is sexual anarchy. This is Dionysus.[179] The liberation of the spirit through sexual pleasure – dance, drugs, music, alcohol, self-indulgence and self-gratification. To feel good about yourself – to be happy, to let your spirit soar and make a connection with god without the mediation of anyone between you and him. To see the face of god, first-hand. To be your own shaman!

***

Jonathan left and David lit a cigarette. So, what now?

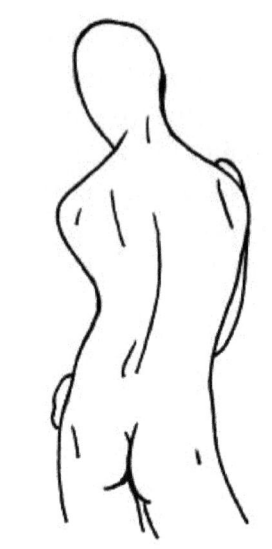

David's Sketch of Jonathan

---

[178] In 1861 sodomy (the act of male-to-male penetrative sex) was punishable by ten years (to life) of penal servitude (forced labour).
[179] *See* Appendix VIII.

Chapter Seven - Separation

10.36 p.m.   Thursday, 17th July 2003.

It's night. David's stood at the bus stop waiting. He checks his watch and shuffles about under shelter, then Carol arrives and the world seems to turn black and white.[180]

He smiles as she approaches. In her hand she has a suitcase.

David   I've been waiting.

Carol   I nearly didn't come.

He smiles nervously.

David   I thought as much.

Carol   I love you.

David   I love you too.

They kissed, like in those old black and white movies…

---

[180] Like *Brief Encounter* (the classic 1945 movie by director David Lean, based on the play *Still Life* by Noel Coward) with her as Celia Johnson and him as Trevor Howard. In the movie Celia Johnson chooses her husband over the 'brief encounter' with Trevor Howard – a man she meets at her local railway station.

Was this real?

His lips are so soft when he kisses her. She feels like she's being lifted out of herself.

***

When he's not there she thinks about him – he fills her days, and when she knows he's coming round she spends the whole day getting ready for him. He makes her feel like she's sixteen again.

I don't think I ever was sixteen before.

And when he held her – naked in his arms – her body felt like silk. Like a silk tablecloth on the polished surface of her body. She is radiant, loving, passionate.

***

He is so different from me. I was brought up in a world that smelt like a chip pan and Sunday roasts, onion gravy and tinned peas. In those days they boiled the life out of everything until it was tasteless. You could tell what day it was by the food on the table - steak and kidney, shepherd's pie - it was all heavy and brown, on heavy brown tables. That was life - functional, flavourless, tinned and brown.

***

I've been waiting for this moment for so long. You don't know what you've done for me. I feel like a young girl again. But why me? Why not someone more your own age?

I don't know. Who plans love with regard to age or time? Things like this happen. We're not meant to question them. We just have to live by what we know.

For that moment she was Celia Johnson. She smelt of *Lux* soap and the bedding box. He was Rick Blaine to her Ilsa.[181] And like Ilsa she had to step on the plane.

Nothing lasts forever. Except for books. They sit on shelves collecting dust. Covers all beaten and faded by the sun.

Will you put me away like a book, Mummy dear?

I might do.

Inanimate objects deserve to be beaten. But the noise? Sound travels at night. But in her bed, she turns again. Back into the land of dreams, a restless night again.

I think I believed in God once.

---

[181] Rick Blaine was the character played by Humphrey Bogart in, the classic 1942 movie, *Casablanca* – the character Ilsa Lund Laszio was played by Ingrid Bergman. The final scene between Ilsa and Rick sees her leaving the love of her life (Rick) to be with her husband (Victor). A morality tale of duty before self.

Chapter Eight – Day

9.36 a.m.   Friday, 18th July 2003.

Another morning.

Mother   Ready for your wash?

She asked, shovelling him out of his bed.

What a dream I had, I dreamed...

...Keep still.

He could hear her!

Jon could hear his mother's thoughts. He jolted in his chair.

I wish you'd keep bloody still.

He can hear the frustration in her tone.

Mum! Mum! Listen to me...

But she couldn't hear him.

You mucky little bastard. I should have you put in a Home.

And now he wished that he couldn't hear her. His spasms became violent, how long had she been thinking this? How much of her caring had been a fucking lie?

Mother What's the matter, Jonathan? Mummy rubbing too hard?

Don't want to hear this. I don't want to hear any more.

He felt hate and fear – and a zillion other emotions without names. They hit him like bullets. He wanted to plug up his ears.

Mother What's the matter with you?

I wish you were dead. I wish you'd just die in your sleep. I want to be free. I want to be with him…

And her wish came true in part. David appeared at the door.

Jon *What are you doing? You shouldn't come when I'm like this.*

There was panic in his voice. He wasn't supposed to see him like this. He wasn't supposed to know him in this place.

Carol *To bathe in his smile and be warmed by his body.*

Jon *David?*

But he didn't seem to notice him.

David *I love you, Carol.*

Inside Jonathan screamed a scream that blew-out his heart. The pain was like somebody had just ripped out his stomach with their bare hands. Jonathan had known pain, but this, this pain was too big for one person to cope with. His body convulsed into fits. He squirmed like a maggot being fried in hot oil. He wished he could move, he wished he had the physical ability to hold himself, to put his head in his hands and cry, but he hadn't. All he could do was sit and feel every last barb of his pain, silently, anonymously, invisibly. As always.

Mother   What is the matter with you, will you keep still!

Jon   *Not with her.*

But David couldn't hear. And the pain that he thought couldn't get any worse – just did!

David   *Put him in a Home and come with me, Carol.*

Jonathan   NO! Not you!

His world blew apart. Fractured into a million pieces. Like the windscreen of a car – his head battering through the glass – it could never be put back, never be fixed, it was fucked. He was fucked, it was all fucked!

Mother   If you're going to be like this then you can stay dirty. Nobody loves dirty little boys.

***

David could see Jon was upset.

David   What's the matter?

Jon tried to hold it in. But couldn't any longer.

Jon   *(through his tears)* You know what's the matter. My mother? Enjoy fucking her, did you?

He grabbed David by his throat and slammed him into the wall. He could see the hate in Jon's eyes. He could feel the pressure of his grip against his neck.

David pushed him back and caught his breath.

David   Listen to me! Just listen will you. I can't help being her fantasy as well. I can't help what goes on in her head.

Jon could feel the physical pain of the words. He felt the physical wrenching of his body. He lent against the wall and cried. Sliding down he huddled – a child – a helpless weeping bundle.

Jon   *(through his tears)* But I love you.

David   So does she.

His voice was calm, emotionless, matter-of-fact.

Jon   *(crying)* So I either share you, or get tortured every time she dreams you – is that what you're saying?

David   I'm sorry.

Jon   *(crying)* Either way I lose.

David didn't speak. At that moment Jon hated him. He found a composure within himself and his tears stopped.

Jon   How long has she been seeing you?

David still didn't answer. In fact, he seemed to look straight through him.

Jon   Have you slept with her?

David   Why are you doing this to yourself?

Jon   How many times?

David wasn't going to answer and Jon took this to mean 'too many times to tell you' and the tears came again.

Jon   *(crying with sheer anger)* Why didn't you tell me?

But how could he? That's how fantasies work. They're private, confidential. More secret than a confessional, and from time to time we share the same fantasies. That's how it works.

***

And then he was back with his mother.[182]

Mother   We don't look very happy today, do we?

He seethed.

I hate you.

He wanted to torture her. He wanted to take meat skewers and pierced her eyes, her breasts, her vagina. He wanted to dig them in and gouge out pieces of her flesh – to see her blood wash down her as she screams out in pain…

> Frustration
> locked inside a skin
> he cannot tear away from
> bound and gagged
> he kicks and fights against his prison
> but shackles bind him
> tie him to this place
> this purgatory
> this here and now.

Mother   Ready for something to eat?

You could have had anyone, but you had to take him. He was mine. The only thing that was ever truly mine.

---

[182] See the concept of ksana in Appendix V.

He felt her laughing inside.

Mother We'll just put your bib on.

And yet another humiliating action.

Why can't you hear me? Why must it only be me that suffers?

And an eternity of pain began.

Carol *Are you there?*

And David answers.

I'm here.

And he was there again. Approaching him, like a hot poker being brought to his eye.

Don't do this. David, please don't do this to me.

His voice – a whispered, whimpering beg.

David *I'm sorry, Jon.*

Carol *What's the matter? What are you saying sorry to Jonathan for?*

She was confused. David just looked at her.

Jonathan *Tell her.*

Carol *David?*

Jonathan *Tell her!*

David *He can hear everything we say.*

Carol   *What?*

Jonathan twitches his hand in response to her question.

Mother   Jonathan?

And for a moment she said nothing as she took in the information.

Jon   *Tell her. Don't deny me! Not like this.*

Then the full horror of the situation is realised as she replays the conversation she's just had with David.

Mother   Oh my god!

David   *And there's something else.*

Carol   *(she couldn't take any more) No! I don't want to hear any more.*

It was as if her brain was overloading – or if she didn't hear it then it wouldn't exist.

David   *He knows about us.*

Carol   *There's nothing to know.*

David   *That's not all...*

But he couldn't bring himself to say any more.

Jon   *(angrily) Tell her!*

He couldn't see why she should be spared the truth.

David   *I've been his fantasy too.*

Carol   *I see.*

David   No, I don't think you do.

He thought about his words – this was the best he could manage.

David   You see, I've been his lover too!

Carol   (through her nervous giggle) What do you mean, his lover?

David   Just that – his lover.

There was nothing. No reaction. No histrionics. Nothing.

Carol   I don't believe you!

Tears began to well in her eyes as she spoke.

You're just making it up. I don't know why you're trying to hurt me like this… Or why you're bringing him into all this.

David   Carol, it's true.

Carol   It can't be! Look at him.

David   When he's with me he's not like that. He's physically quite normal.

Carol   (in disgust) 'Normal'?

She knew he was lying.

Carol   He's a cripple. He has no sexual feelings whatsoever – it's impossible!

David   Then why don't you ask him yourself?

She hadn't looked at Jonathan since the nightmare had begun.

Carol	He doesn't communicate. If he could, don't you think I'd know. I am his mother after all.

David	When was the last time you tried?

Her anger dies down as she thinks…

Then try again.

She finally looks at her twisted son.

Mother	Jonathan?

Jonathan	Mother?

And she hears him. What happened next is up to you. Did they lose him? Did they share him? Beyond this moment all is possible…

Chapter Nine - Unknown

8.57 p.m.   Friday, 22nd August 2003.

Manchester was hosting Europride[183] – the biggest gay festival in Europe. Canal Street was filled with market stalls and the bars were full to capacity.

To be allowed onto the street you had to buy a wristband.

A young man waited by the barrier...

    And he waited...

        And waited...

            And waited...

Was his hair brown or blond? In the shadow world everything is possible.[184]

***

---

[183] From Friday 22nd August to Monday 25th August, 2003.
[184] An absolute is only the limit of our conception.

If we shadows have offended,
Think but this, and all is mended,
That you have but slumber'd here
While these visions did appear.
And this weak and idle theme,
No more yielding but a dream,
Gentles, do not reprehend:
If you pardon, we will mend.
And, as I'm an honest Puck,[185]
If we have unearned luck
Now to 'scape the serpent's tongue,
We will make amends ere long;
Else the Puck a liar call:
So, good night unto you all.
Give me your hands, if we be friends,
And Robin shall restore amends.

Puck's last speech from *A Midsummer Night's Dream*
- by William Shakespeare, 1596.[186]

---

[185] Puck – a shape-shifting hob-goblin who misleads mortals (also referred to as Robin Good-fellow). Often linked to the ancient Greek god Pan, the goat-footed deity, who seduced young men at noon – also associated with Christ and Dionysus.
[186] Act V, Scene 1. *See* **Further Crippled.**

Appendix I: Odin

Odin (meaning *'rager'*) was also known by the names Wotan and Woden.[187] He was the Nordic Germanic god associated with Shamanism, storms, battles, and sacrifice. His name signified *'fury'*, *'wildness'* and *'inspiration'*. He ruled the moment of no return: the point where the spear is cast and the arrow leaves the bow, the instant when orgasm is unstoppable and inspiration begins. His honorary names included Bileyg,[188] Galgagram,[189] Sidfodir,[190] and Valfodr.[191] He was believed to a shape-changer,[192] able to enter any place or situation he chose, even to overcome death. But his main function was as lawgiver and ruler of gods and mortals. It was believed that Odin took brave heroes, who were killed in battle to Valhalla,[193] with the assistance of his warrior-maidens the Valkyries.

This band of dead warriors was known as *The Wild Hunt* and the sound of their approach was thought to herald death. The *Berserkir*[194] were these heroes, a frenzied group of shape-shifting warriors with the properties of werewolves.

Odin was one of the sons of Bor,[195] father of the gods. He and his brothers Vili and Ve killed the frost-giant Ymir,[196] and used his body

---

[187] From where we get the name *Wednesday*, meaning *'Stronghold of the god Woden'*.
[188] *The Shifty-eyed.*
[189] *The Gallows Lord.*
[190] *The Victory-giver.*
[191] *Father of the Slain.*
[192] An ability to change his form into other things.
[193] The place where the dead heroes would feast and tell stories until the final days of judgement, known as *Ragnarok*, when the forces of good and evil would finally do battle for the supremacy of the earth.
[194] Meaning *'bear-shirts'* or *Ulfhedna*, meaning *'wolf-shirts'*.
[195] Son of Buri, the first human. Bor was married to the ice-giantess Bestla.
[196] Father of the ice giants.

to create the physical universe.[197] He searched perpetually for knowledge and used his shape-changing abilities to discover what life was like as many different things.[198] He understood the languages of all creatures, and had two raven-servants, Huginn (*'thought'*) and Muninn (*'memory'*). Each day Huginn would fly around the world of the living, and Muninn would do the same around the world of the dead, and every evening they perched on his shoulders and would tell him what they had seen.

Odin often concealed his identity so that he could wander the world. He once asked the Norns[199] to drink from the Well of Urd, which gave wisdom to one of the roots of *Yggdrasil*. As payment he plucked out one of his eyes. During this experience he stabbed himself with his own spear and hung himself, dead, on *Yggdrasil* for nine days and nine nights, and let the dew of the tree seep into his bones. This event brought him another title, Hangagud, *'The Hanging God'*.

---

[197] Then the brothers disappear from mythology as Odin becomes ruler.
[198] Including smoke, water, insects and leaves.
[199] The three sisters that tended the Well of Urd, which watered *Yggdrasil*, the Tree of Knowledge.

Appendix II: The Runes

The word *'rune'* comes from the German *'raunen'* meaning *'secret'* or *'mystery'*. The Norse god Odin payed for this *'secret'* with one of his eyes, and in return he was given the gift of their *'mystery'*. Casting runes is a method of divination[200] using twenty-four marked stones, known as the Elder Futhork.[201] This set of stones consists of three *'suits'* of eight symbols, or *'aettirs'*, and a blank rune known as *Wyrd*.

As with any oracular device it is not what *it* does for us, but what *we* ourselves bring to *it*. In this respect the runes are unique, and as part of the acquiring of the runes, you must put part of your energy in their creation. You can find the stones, or you can craft them from clay or wood. You can even make special sets for specific *'castings'* or events. In doing this, the creativity of the maker *'charges'* their personality into the oracle.[202]

If you find the stones it is best to choose pebbles that are of the same size and shape. Those smoothed by water have a better feel and connection with the natural forces that have helped to shape them. You can *'neutralise'* and *'purify'* residual energy from acquired or found objects by washing them in a rock, or sea salt solution.

When creating the marks on your runes, either in clay, wood or paint, think about the meaning of each symbol. Charge the oracle as you create it. Force your energy into the object as you give it form. This connection is very important and is the key to working with the

---

[200] Prediction.
[201] So called because *'f'*, *'u'*, *'t'*, *'h'*, *'o'*, *'r'* and *k'* are the first six letters in the runic alphabet from which the runes originate their symbols.
[202] And, thus, *'tuning'* the instrument with your energy and resonance.

runes. As you give it your energy it becomes an extension of your own thought.

Once you have created your runes keep them safe in a cloth bag, made from natural fibres, and store them in a wooden box. To keep them charged with your energy allow no-one but yourself to handle them. If you require others to touch them remember to cleanse their energy from them by washing them, as mentioned above.

At all times treat the oracle with humility and respect. On their own the runes can do nothing, they merely allow you to open up your own perception of the truth, promoting your own intuitive thought. The relationship you develop with the runes depends upon you.

Using the Runes

Shake the runes in the bag and think about the question you wish to ask them. Then take out three stones and shake them in your hands. Throw the stones onto a table and place them from left to right in a row, in the order in which they fell. These runes represent the past, the present and the future, and are read from left to right.

First is the past or what was. Second is the present or the action that should be taken. Third is the future or what will be.[203]

The Aeittir Cloth

This is a casting cloth marked with a circle divided into three segments. The first segment is *Freya*, that refers to matters of love, creativity and happiness. The second section is *Hagal*, looks at business, achievement, success, and money (the things we desire). The third division, *Tiu*, is responsible for our mind and the spirit (such as our life philosophy and ethics).

---

[203] There are other rune casts and a great many books on the subject. One of the best is *The Book of Runes*, by Ralph Blum, published by Oracle Books, California, 1982.

For a more detailed reading of a question cast the runes onto the cloth and read them from within the associated segments. Each rune will then correspond to these specific areas of interest.

The Meaning of the Runes

When runes are cast some lay face down, some face up, some lay reversed. The positions of these runes are important and are interpreted according to the following guidelines:

REYA'S AETTIR

FEOH / FEHU, meaning *'cattle'* or possessions.

Feoh is the first letter in the old German alphabet. It is equivalent to *'F'* and ruled by the Moon and Venus. The key words for this rune are physical and financial needs, such as property, money, promotion and self-esteem.
Face up this rune is about what we posses, or own. It is a rune of good fortune and abundance, and financial strength in future. In earlier times this would have been linked to fertility and livestock, and is linked to reward through effort. A victory after struggle.
Face down this rune forecasts the loss of property or social standing. It represents a failure of some kind, maybe greed or stupidity.
In reverse the rune symbolises a matter that is beyond repair.

UR / URUZ, meaning *'Aurochs'*[204] or strength.

Ur is the alphabetic equivalent of *'U'* and is ruled by the planet Mars. The key words for this rune are based around sexuality, virility and passion.
Face up this is the rune of physical strength and potential. It denotes a period of great energy and health. Like the creature it represents, *Ur*, is about freedom, tenacity, and courage. A chance to prove oneself and shoulder new responsibilities.
Face down and the rune tells of domination by others; weakness, and illness. Once again, like the Aurochs, it could herald a period of brutality, callousness, and violence.
Reversed the rune depicts a lost opportunity, impaired judgement and obstacles. In effect, the rune tells us to temporarily abandon whatever it is we are engaged upon until another time.

---

[204] A wild ox or bison.

Þ THORN / THURISAZ, meaning *'thorn'* or a gateway.

The phonetic equivalent of this rune is *'th'* and ruled by the planet Jupiter. Key words here are those of hardship, pain and discipline. For it is only through these times that we can truly hope to learn about our inner-selves.

Face up this rune shows us the coming destruction or conflict of a situation. This could denote a tendency towards change or violent male impulses.

Face down and the rune is about danger, vulnerability, and betrayal. This puts us on guard of lies, malice and hatred.

Reversed this rune warns us against a hasty decision and the cost of ignoring the potential hazards highlighted by good advice.

ᚠ ANSUR / OSS / ANSUZ / OS, meaning *'the mouth'* or signals.

This rune is linked to Odin and is the alphabetic equivalent of *'A'*. As a messenger rune it is ruled by the planet Mercury and its key words are justice, balance and clairvoyance.

Face up the rune is revealing. It evokes the nature of communication and inspiration, the power of words and names.

Face down and the rune indicates misunderstanding and delusion. A time when we could be at the mercy of somebody else's selfish advice.

Reversed this rune denotes the mischievous god Loki, and the danger and disaster he brings. These negative influences make it impossible to see the truth and urges you to take a second opinion in matters of importance. Be aware of a broken promise and do not divulge information at this time.

ᚱ RAD / RIT / RAIDO, meaning *'cartwheel'* or a journey.

The alphabetic equivalent of this rune is *'R'* and its ruler is Mercury. Key words associated with *Rad* are those linked to progress, change, and destiny. As well as travel and movement from one place to another.

Face up the rune has a sense of change about it, either in lifestyle or setting. It's a rune of changing perception and decision.

Face down and it becomes a rune of crisis and stasis, the sense of dislocation and imprisonment are felt here. A feeling that we are stuck or caged in.

Reversed the rune often speaks of an unexpected journey in difficult circumstances, possibly a friend or relative may be ill. This rune throws our plans into chaos and is not a time to take on new ventures.

ᚲ KAON / KEN / KAUNAZ / KENAZ / KANO, meaning *'torch'* or opening.

This rune's alphabetic partner is *'C'* and is ruled by Mars and the Sun. Key phrases here are, those of creativity, inspiration, wisdom, and solution.

Face up this is the oracle of knowledge and new vision. It is an empowering rune full of fresh hope and positive energy. A fire rune linked to the ancient sun cults of springtime and fertility.
Face down the rune denotes a time of instability and disillusionment, the feeling of hopelessness and despair.
Reversed this rune is a symbol of hibernation and the possible end of a relationship.

X GIFU / GEOFU / GYFU / GEBO, meaning *'gift'* or partnership.

Seen at the letter *'G'* and ruled by the planet Venus, the key words for this rune are generosity, unexpected good fortune and relationships.
Face up this rune represent gifts, as both sacrifice and generous acts. In this rune there is a sense of balance and equality in relation to exchanges.
Face down the rune carries a sense of greed and loneliness, dependence and one-sided generosity. The negative aspects of partnership and giving.
This glyph has no reverse.

P WUNNA / WYNN / WYN, meaning *'glory'* or joy.

The letter here is *'W'* and it's ruling planets are Venus and Saturn. Its key words are recognition, success and reward. The contentment one gets when one has achieved goals. This is the rune of an artisan or worker.
Face up the rune indicates the feeling of pleasure and comfort, prosperity and fellowship. A harmonious rune that means success and recognition of worth.
Face down and the rune means sorrow, strife, and rage.
Reversed this could indicate the coming of unpleasant news, with the negative aspects of Saturn introducing an aspect of deception.

HAGAL'S AETTIR

N HAGAL / HAGALL / HAGALAZ, meaning *'hail'* or disruption.

The letter *'H'* represents this rune, ruled by Saturn. Its key words are disaster, destruction and sudden loss.
Face up this is the rune of uncontrolled forces, leading to completion and inner harmony.
Face down the rune predicts natural disasters, loss and hardship.
This glyph has no reverse meaning.

✝ NAUT / NIED, meaning *'necessity'* or constraint.

Linked to the letter *'N'* and ruled by Saturn this glyph's key phrases are discontentment, hardship and responsibility. Frustration and insurmountable obstacles.

Face up this puts us on alert for delays and resistance. But the power this there to overcome it, through endurance and determination. This rune calls for patience and the facing fears.

Face down the rune highlights our constraint and distress, caused by toil and drudgery. It also indicates the emotional hunger that often caused by these feelings.

Reversed this rune warns us of potentially disastrous courses of action.

IS / ISA, meaning *'ice'* or standstill.

The alphabetic symbol of this rune is *'I'* and its planet is Jupiter. The key words associated with this rune are withdrawal, stagnation and reflection.

Face up the rune indicates a challenge or frustration. This is a time to turn inwards and wait for clarity. As the earth sleeps under ice and waits for the sun, so must you.

Face down the rune depicts treachery and deceit, betrayal and plots.

This glyph has no reverse meaning.

YER / JARA, meaning *'year'* or harvest.

The alphabetic equivalent is *'Y'* and is ruled by the planet Mercury. Its key words are those of change. The yearly cycle of reward, productivity and development.

Face up this is a rune that calls for the realisation of time, that results will be reaped for earlier efforts. The rejoicing that comes after a period of stagnation.

This rune is the same face up or face down, and has no reverse.

YR, meaning *'yew tree'* or defence.

The phonetic equivalent of this rune is *'EL'* and is ruled by Jupiter. Key phrases include, change and initiation. This is a time to confront one's fears. A turning point, followed by transformation.

Face up the rune shows us the possibility of achieving goals. It is a symbol of strength and dependability.

Face down and the rune alerts us to confusion and an inability to overcome the current issues that face us. Remember that a bow made of yew can bend.

This glyph has no reversed meaning.

PEORTH / PERTH, meaning *'a dice cup'* or hearth.

The letter associated with this rune is *'P'* and is ruled by the planet Mars. The key words to this rune are, change, rebirth and new beginnings.

Face up this rune represents initiation and the knowledge of one's destiny. It relates to the feminine aspects of our psyche and is a rune of secret matter, and hidden things.

Face down the rune warns against addiction and the lack of understanding, and death.
Reversed this rune predicts disappointment and the negative aspects that can befall us when we take a gamble.

ᛉ AQUIZI / EOLTH / ALGIZ, meaning *'elk'* or protection.

The phonetic equivalents of this sign are the *'X'* and *'Z'*. The rune is ruled by the planets Jupiter and Venus. The key words are defence, warning and support.
Face up this is a rune of protection or shielding. It urges us to shelter ourselves and others.
Face down this rune denotes a hidden danger or a warning of some description.
Reversed it tells us of exposure and vulnerability, and that we are without protection, and may be being used by others for their own ends.

ᛋ SIG / SIGEL / SOWELU, meaning *'Sun'* or wholeness.

The alphabetical equivalent of this rune is *'S'*, and it is ruled by the Sun. Key words here are those of success, fertility and health.
Face up this calls on the life force of the Sun, bringing with it success, honour and health. This is a time when a positive change may occur.
Face down we are made aware of false goals and bad advice. We are warned about the illusion of success and the evils of vanity.
This glyph has no reversed meaning.

TIU'S AETTIR

ᛏ TIU / TIR / TEIWAZ, meaning *'Tiu'* or warrior.

The letter associated with this rune is *'T'* and its planet is Mars. Words associated with this sign are duty, self-sacrifice and conflict.
Face up, this rune is one of honour, justice, and authority. It wills its reader to look for truth and the strength in self-sacrifice.
Face down this rune shows the blocking of energy and mental paralysis. The in-balance between achievement and sacrifice.
Reversed the rune indicates that in a sexual relationship has no future. The prospect of infidelity and lack of commitment are indicated.

ᛒ BIRCA / BEORC / BERKANA, meaning *'birch tree'* or growth.

The letter here is *'B'* and the ruling planets are the Moon and Jupiter. Words associated with this rune are healing, fertility, and new beginnings. This is the rune of conception and plenty.
Face up this rune represents birth, fertility, and regeneration. It is the power of spring, and the promise of new beginnings. A time for love and birth.

Face down can denote family or domestic problems, and the anxiety about someone close.
Reversed this rune indicates a misfortunate aspect to birth or fertility.

ᛖ EH / EOH / EHWAZ, meaning *'horse'* or movement.

The alphabetical equivalent is *'E'* and its ruling body is that of Mercury. Words related to this rune are those of motion and transportation.
Face up this rune tells us of transportation or movement of some description. It is a rune of change, but a change for the better. Of progress and development.
Face down the rune signifies a craving for change, and a feeling of restlessness. Even face down this is not a negative rune.
Reversed this sign represents travel over water or the sea, or a change brought about through disruption.

ᛗ MAN / MANN / MANNAZ, meaning *'man'* or The Self.

The alphabetic sign for this rune is *'M'* and its ruler is Saturn. Associated words to this rune are family, community, and those things related to people.
Face up this is the rune of *'the self'*, the individual, and singularity. Our attitude towards others and their attitudes towards ourselves are also highlighted here.
Face down this rune warns against a period of self-delusion and the feelings of depression.
Reversed, this rune denotes the fall of man, false truths and the desire for sensual pleasures.

ᛚ LAGU / LAGUZ, meaning *'water'* or flow.

The letter associated with this rune is *'L'* and its ruling body is the Moon. Key words include emotion, thoughts and intuition.
Face up, this rune is a rune of dreams and fantasies. The unknown and the hidden are also muted at. Like water, this is about the flow of intuition, and psychic matters.
Face down the rune warns of a period of confusion and poor judgement.
Reversed this is an unfortunate rune. The Moon here indicates trickery and disaster, if the present course of action is continued.

ᛜ ING / INGUZ, meaning *'people'* or fertility.

The phonetic equivalent of this rune is *'ng'* and its ruling power is Venus. Key words associated with this rune are work, productivity and connection with the land.
Face up this is calls for a resting stage in your life. A time of relief with no feelings of anxiety. A time to tie-up loose ends and the freedom to move on.
Face down the rune indicates impotence, stagnation and labour.

⊗ ODAL / OTHILA, meaning *'inherited property'* or separation.

The alphabetic correspondent to this rune is *'O'* and its key words are those related to property, land, inheritance and the home.
Face up this rune is about possessions, the home and what is truly important to you. Heritage and fundamental values are also denoted here.
Face down the rune represent the loss of friends or family, or of being homelessness and cut off from one's roots.

⋈ DAG / DAEG, meaning *'day'* or breakthrough.

The letter associated with this rune is *'D'* and its related words are those of happiness, fulfilment of a lifestyle and satisfaction.
Face up this is a rune associated with a breakthrough, or awakening. It shows an awareness, as daylight clarifies and a period in which to plan begins.
Face down the rune shows us the completion or ending of something. A time when we have come full circle.

▢ WYRD, the Blank Rune.

It's meaning is that of fate and change. It represents the unavoidable and inevitable.

Appendix III: Collective Consciousness

The Hindus believe in a mystical repository of all knowledge called the *Akasic Records*. This is a huge matrix[205] of every thought and feeling, every memory and idea that has ever been. Throughout the centuries medicine men, and religious teachers, have claimed their wisdom[206] has been given to them from some *'vast eternal knowledge'*. Cultures with no physical means of communication – separated by thousands of miles and insurmountable obstacles have drawn startlingly similar conclusions to esoteric mysteries. The psychologist Carl Gustav Jung[207] called this phenomenon the *Collective Unconscious*.

As individuals we dream, as a society we create myths; this is the basis of our collective unconscious. Our fantasies, collectively, become legends. These myths and legends patch into our dreams, and vice versa, creating a host of symbolic and metaphoric archetypes we all share[208] irrespective of race, religion or cultural divides.

***

Our senses are ways of accessing and interacting with different portions of the electromagnetic spectrum of energy, either directly as in touch or indirectly as in sight[209] – and everything we experience

---

[205] The Hebrew *Kabbalah* is such a system - of interlocking pigeonholes for data organisation.
[206] The Bible and The Koran are claimed to have been written by God through man.
[207] **Carl Gustav Jung** *(1875–1966)* was a pupil and friend of Sigmund Freud – the founder of modern psychoanalysis.
[208] Such as demons and angels.
[209] Matter is only *'sticky'* energy.

through our bodies is translated into electrochemical signals that are sent to the brain.[210]

Like a modem on a computer that connects it to the outside world. Our bodies collect data for us to analysed and sorted, and eventually stored as memories, and as a computer holds a history of its past functions, so do we. In that respect we are soft machines.

Deleted information on a computer is still there – held within its memory – most of the time we can't access it, unless we know the correct procedure. The SIM card[211] in a mobile phone also holds the ghosts of deleted text messages that the normal phone's functions can't access[212] – just because *we* can't retrieve them doesn't mean they are not still there.

If our body dies, we become *'disconnected'* from our physical world. The modem is switched off. If the brain (our hard drive) is corrupted the information could be lost. So, does the brain have a back-up system? Is this what the *Akasic Records* are – our brain downloads?

Anything that affects our neural system creates a radio wave. This is in essence a broadcast. If we could modulate this broadcast during the moment of death (when there is a massive adrenal surge in our bodies) or when we feel we are in mortal danger (and we have, what some call, an *Out Of Body Experience*), then maybe we could download our minds to another place.

If we accept that this could be possible – and we can broadcast of our memories – then we can also, maybe, receive memories. If this is true, then in each of us is deeply buried in the memories of every other person on the planet – as well as all the memories of those who are now dead.[213]

***

---

[210] Every thought we have changes the neural balance of the brain.
[211] **SIM** stands for Subscriber Identity Module.
[212] The police and mobile phone companies do have the technology to retrieve over 100 deleted text messages from a cell phone SIM card.
[213] Our own minds could be the repository of the *Akasic Records*.

When we die, we weigh 21 grams less than when we were alive… Why? What is that 21 grams? Is it our *'spirit'*?[214] In some cultures the *'spirit'* is believed to jump into another vessel.[215] If that is true why do we not all remember past lives? Maybe we do; maybe like the SIM card we just cannot access the ghosts of our past because we do not need them. Why hold onto information about a *past* life? Surely, we only need to store in our hard-drive the information we need for this life.[216] Why fill up our memory with stuff we do not need?[217] Just because we cannot access the information with our normal functions does not mean it is not there.

---

[214] For want of a better word.

[215] Reincarnation.

[216] A great deal of the brain's function is taken up with facial recognition. How many faces do we see in a lifetime? How many images do we have to store in our brains? How many more would it be if we had hundreds of lifetimes-worth of information stored up (information we didn't need - memories that have nothing to do with this present incarnation)?

[217] And of course, many death experiences are traumatic – do we really want to have that experience still lurking at the back of our heads?

Appendix IV: Michelangelo

Michelangelo Buonarroti was born on 6th March, 1475, in the small town of Caprese, in the Apennine mountain region of rural Tuscany. Legend has it, that when he was born Mercury and Venus were in the House of Jupiter.[218] He was only six years old when his mother died and by the age of fifteen, he was in the service of The Medici family. The Medicis were successful bankers and the most influential family in Florence.[219] It was during this time he began to sculpt.[220]

Michelangelo was obsessed with perfection.[221] His competitive nature drove him to achieve greatness within his own field. His best-known work is that of *David*[222] – the colossal sculpture, whose copy now stands in the Louvre, Paris. The original took him two and a half years to complete,[223] and stands 5 metres tall. Carved from one single block of forty-year-old, flawless marble. Michelangelo said of the sculpting: *'David is imprisoned inside the block of marble all I have to do is release him.'*

---

[218] A fabrication by Michelangelo, who re-invented himself into a divine genius and child prodigy. *He was the first artist ever to sign his own work (such was the belief in his own genius).*
[219] The Medici family were the de facto rulers of Florence, and the greatest art patrons of the Renaissance period.
[220] Michelangelo was one of the greatest marble sculptors of all time.
[221] He had his nose broken in a fight, leaving him deformed and *'ugly'* – making his pursuit of perfection even more important in his artistic work.
[222] David was a warrior-king and prophet, famous for slaying the Philistine warrior Goliath. In the *Book of Samuel*, in *The Old Testament*, David is loved by Jonathan, the son of King Saul, and David loves him *'passing the love of women' (Old Testament: II Samuel: 1:26).*
[223] Finished in 1501.

David is a depiction of sheer Renaissance beauty, based on a classical form.[224] The sculpture shows David naked. He stands facing the viewer, exposed and vulnerable.[225] Yet, at the same time, strong and defiant.

Michelangelo used a reverse perspective in the creation of his sculpture, adding to the magnitude of the image that stands before you. His head and hands – representing intelligence and physical strength – are proportionally larger than the rest of the body, emphasising the two important qualities of the god-like David.[226]

In his studies Michelangelo[227] used *The Golden Ratio* to proportion *David* into a depiction of beauty. *The Golden Ratio* - sometimes called *The Golden Mean* or *Divine Proportion* - is the numerical formula of beauty. The ratio appears in nature and architecture all the time, and equates the length to width of approximately 1 to 1.618.[228] This ratio is visually pleasing and relates to *The Fibonacci Sequence* - which states that if you divide two consecutive numbers in the sequence (1, 1, 2, 3, 5, 8, 13, 21...[229]) the answer is always an approximation of phi. *The Ratio* is found in the proportions of the face and body, the pitch of a DNA spiral, the structure of a mollusc shell or a sunflower. Trees, sonnets, widescreen televisions, Gothic cathedrals and credit cards all contain *The Ratio* – the magical number of beauty.

The money Michelangelo received for the sculpture of *David* was more than Leonardo da Vinci[230] earned in his who life time. Michelangelo died on 18th February, 1564.

---

[224] The Classical Period relating to the ancient civilisations of Greece and Rome.
[225] '*Exposed*' to physical attack, open to temptation and censure.
[226] One of Michelangelo's greatest loves – and the inspiration for a host of sonnets – was the young nobleman Tommaso de'Cavalieri *(born in 1509)*.
[227] And Leonardo da Vinci.
[228] The exact measurement is 1.618,033,989.
[229] 1 + 1 = 2, 1 + 2 = 3, 2 + 3 = 5, 3 + 5 = 8, 5 + 8 = 13, 8 + 13 = 21 and so on...
[230] **Leonardo da Vinci** *(1452-1519)* created one of the greatest works of art of all time, the *Mona Lisa*. His notebooks and journals also show that his studies in the sciences – especially in the field of anatomy and biology – were in advance of many of his generation. Da Vinci also visualised the first flying machines, the first

Appendix V: The Alexander Technique

The Alexander Technique is a method of *'organising your sensations of movement'*, by becoming more aware of your inner and outer worlds through your body. Frederick Matthias Alexander,[231] discovered that our posture has an important effect on the way we move and behave[232] and that the way we *'use'* ourselves affects how well we function.

We learn *'bad habits'* from the moment we begin to move and this effects our posture. Maintaining an upright posture represents one of the basic principals in Alexander's theory. It is this upright posture – or *'alignment'* of the spinal column – that prevents the problems caused by bad posture habits. Using our conscious will to gain control of our bodies, it is possible to grow and develop. But this can only come about through change.

When we get our posture right, we can see striking improvements in our mood, blood pressure, breathing, depth of sleep, and mental alertness.

---

submarine and the first parachute. He was an architect, musician, engineer and poet. At the age of fifty he adopted a ten-year-old boy called Salai, whom he nicknamed *'Little Devil'* – they remained together for 26 years.

[231] Born in Austria, 20th January, 1869.

[232] In *Shu* massage, manipulation of points along the spine can effect changes in the rest of the body by altering the flow of energy (as in acupuncture) - The point at the base of the skull is good for relieving stress, headaches and hangovers. The top of the spine can relieve symptoms of colds, flu and help you when you're feeling *'under the weather'*. The 13th vertebrae (the spine bone) helps with breathing and is good after being in a smoky atmosphere. The 15th vertebrae is good for the heart and the day after a night's clubbing. The base of the spine can help build up energy in the body and strengthen the back. *NB: When massaging the back be careful not to exert too much pressure or you could cause severe damage.*

When moving, *'let the neck be free so that the head can go forward and up so that the back can lengthen and widen'* allowing you to follow a clear route. So that when the body is in balance, the fulcrum[233] is in the same vertical line as the centre of gravity. Movement is then the impulse, or flow of energy, from this point in response to a given stimulus, making us move either from or to a given point in space.

---

[233] The pivot at the base of the skull where the spine fits into the head.

Appendix VI: Astral Projection

Astral Projection is the ability to mentally project, or free, a *'spirit'* body from the earthly, physical body, allowing you access to travel to, and through, other realities.

***

Every culture has a concept of an astral dimension,[234] and the thing that stops us from travelling there is our physical body[235] – and our belief in the existence of other dimensions. Our senses are primarily concerned with interacting in a physical environment. Our consciousness tells us this is real because we can physically see, hear, touch and taste it. In other dimensions that are not physical and cannot be seen, heard, touched or tasted – how can we prove they exist? The answer is we cannot.[236]

The science of *Quantum Mechanics*[237] has suggested that there could be parallel universes.[238] These are other realities that run parallel to

---

[234] Such as Heaven.

[235] As we live in a physical world a physical body is the best way to interact with it – but in a world that has no physical presence a non-physical form would be best.

[236] In 1920 the U.S. Congress tried to close the U.S. Patent Office because it believed that *'everything that could be invented had been invented'*.

[237] Quantum Mechanics developed in the late 20th century to account for the physical principles of our world that classical (or *Newtonian*) mechanics could not answer. *Relativity* described the physics of very massive and very fast objects, and *Quantum Mechanics* explains the physics of very small objects. These two fields contradict *Newtonian Mechanics* but still reproduce the same results, as classical physics, when applied to the same principles. [**Sir Isaac Newton** *(1642–1727)* famous for his theories on planetary orbits and gravity, and inventing the reflecting telescope. It is believed that, from 1687 to 1693, he was having a relationship with the Swiss mathematician, Fatio de Duller - when the relationship ended Newton had a nervous breakdown.]

our own reality – for example, when we choose a certain course of action, say based on two choices, in another parallel world the choice we *didn't make in this* reality *was* made in that one.

We are not aware of the other realities because we are only programmed for this one.[239] It is a little bit like trying to access an *Apple Mac* file with *Microsoft Word* – it simply does not show up on the list of files (unless you can change the application[240]). Maybe the feeling of *déjà vu*[241] is a brief glimpse into another dimension. Maybe hauntings, UFOs, hallucinations, Out-of-Body Experiences, dreams, visions, coincidences, the feeling that your friend is going to call just before they do, are all minor glitches in the fabric of time.[242]

***

The mind is often condemned as *'getting in the way'* of things. Meditation is a way of training the mind to focus. Ordinary physical

---

[238] In 1935 Schrödinger, a highly influential figure in *Quantum Mechanics*, published a three-part essay on *The Present Situation in Quantum Mechanics*, in which he posed the famous *'cat paradox'*. This was a *thought experiment* about a cat in a closed box. Was the cat living or dead? The answer being that both universes, one with a dead cat and one with a live cat, seemed to exist in parallel until an observer opened the box.

[239] Can you imagine how confusing it would be to be aware of all the outcomes, for all the decisions we *could have* made in our lifetime? How many choices do we consciously, and subconsciously, make every single day? Sometimes it is bad enough following a single strand of existence, never mind countless variations.

[240] But you have to know it is there before you can look for it and even then, you may not necessarily be able to read the file.

[241] The experience of feeling that a new situation has been experienced before.

[242] One day computers will be so advanced that they will be able to create a *'physical'* virtual space that our human bodies can physically interact with. The movie trilogy *The Matrix* explores this concept in detail. The science of it states that, statistically *'it is more likely'* that we are presently living within a computer-generated matrix than not living in a computer matrix – and the advancement in computer-generated graphics (based on its development over the past 20 years) could create three-dimensional holographic images that are so advanced that they believed themselves to be *'real'*... And, therefore, the odds are *'that the majority of us are computer-generated graphics'*! And so *'glitches in time'* are in fact *'glitches'* in a computer programme – and that ghosts, reincarnation, and anything else you can put down to the esoteric is purely our way of explaining a fault in a computer-generated matrix... This does sound more plausible than the paranormal.

exercise can be used to focus our minds.[243] In Buddhism Mantras[244] (chants) and Mandalas[245] (images) are used to keep the conscious part of our brain busy (on looking at a picture, chanting a prayer or physically doing an activity), allowing our subconscious mind to raise to the surface. Day-dreaming is a form of meditative trance.

Try to imagine a bright red circle in front of you, change its form into a square, and then a cube - a butterfly - an arrow - a man. When you can do this exercise with your eyes open, and still see the images clearly - even in daylight – then you have begun to develop the first steps towards concentration, and the ability to eliminate the mind's distractions.

These are the first steps in meditation.

When we can eliminate the distraction of *'incoming data'* (background noise) that our minds throw at us, we can begin to stretch our perception of time. This is the bases of *'going into a trance'*. Once the trance has been attained the ability to concentrate increases. This is because in a trance the entire mind can be focused on examining just one piece of data at a time. This is known as being in the *'eternal present'* – a moment where *'time'* is non-existent – an experience known as *'stasis'* or *'nonduration'*.

***

Brain activity produces an energy-pattern that we can read as brainwaves; even a thought has a physical analogue. In a *'flash of inspiration'* the brain kicks into a higher gear for a fraction of a second. In meditation a similar *'instant'* can occur. The Buddhist term for this *'instant'* is the *ksana* – which also means *'the favourable moment'* – and any instant may become the *ksana*, illumination can become instantaneous (*eka-ksana*) and usually appears like a flash of light.[246] The *ksana* exists with every other

---

[243] As in yoga.
[244] *Mantra*, from the Sanskrit word, meaning to *'think'* or *'reason'*.
[245] *Mandala*, from the Sanskrit word, *'yantra'* or diagram – *'mandala'* itself originally meant only *'circle'*.
[246] A flash of inspiration.

instant of time – past, present and future.[247] By jumping into *ksana* from the present, you are able to jump off again into any other point in the past or future.[248]

***

What is space anyway?

In trying to describe *'space'* the concept of *'curved space'* was created, by thinking about it as a curved surface (or sphere). This is misleading because space can only be defined by the distance between two points[249] (defined by a straight line) and a *'surface'* is only a mathematical abstraction within actual (three-dimensional) space. You *can always* connect two points on the surface of a physical object by a straight line (by going through it) and properties can only be given to objects that exist *within* space and time.

So you cannot assign any properties to space (or time) as they are the *'outer forms of existence'*.[250]

***

---

[247] Particles carry mass and energy as they move (and are physical objects). Waves carry energy but no mass (such as ripples on water). In *Quantum Mechanics* this distinction between particles and waves is blurred. Things which we think of as particles (like electrons) can act like waves under certain conditions – while things which we think of as waves (like light) can act like particles. Electrons can create wave-like diffraction patterns when they pass through narrow slits, just like water does as it pass through a lock or under a bridge. Thus making a physical object act like a wave, allowing it to be in two places at the same time. The theory of a *dualistic* wave-particle nature of all physical objects (dependent on the physical situation) became established with the publication of a document called *The Compton Effect* [not connected, but interesting that, *Old Compton Street* is the name of the road which hosts London's Soho Gay Scene].

[248] This is thinking about one place and then another. Then thinking about both places being the same – a *ksana* – being in two places at once (or two points in time existing at the same point in time).

[249] And there are no points in space.

[250] And are not three-dimensional.

On 7th June, 1969, Professor I. M. Kogan, Chairman of the Bio-information Section of the Moscow Board of the A. S. Popov Society, in the U.S.S.R., delivered a paper entitled *'The Information Theory Aspect of Telepathy – A New Look at E.S.P.'*.[251] In the paper Kogan stated that *'transmission by the electromagnetic field of biocurrents is possible'* and that science could show how *telepathy*[252] could be scientifically proven.

Scientists have shown that we use around 80% of our brain to stay alive and what we use the remaining 20% for is, at present, mostly unclear. For a brain signal to travel any distance it would need a power source – our brains already produce enough power for this – all we have to learn is how to shift our consciousness to a higher wavelength.

Kogan believes that we can transmit 7 bits of information per second (in dense urban areas) for a distance of around 50 metres (before the transmission decays). The message, the density of population and the distance are all factors in the quality of the transmission.[253]

***

Our physical bodies are made of matter – matter is *'sticky'* energy – and if we alter the basic structure of matter by rearranging elections, protons, neutrons and so on[254] then we can change its properties and its form.

Light travels at 186,279 miles a second. Light is made up of photons. When they travel in space they act like a stream of bullets; when they come into contact with matter they behave like a wave. If we

---

[251] **E.S.P.** (Extra Sensory Perception) – The use of *'sense'* beyond those of sight, sound, touch, smell and taste.
[252] *Telepathy* is the communication between two people – seemingly brain-to-brain – in a way that *'normal'* science cannot explain.
[253] Telepathy does not work on logical concepts such as names and places. We can transmit actions, sensations, emotions, directions – colour, shape, texture – in one-minute intervals. The greater the density of population, the greater the background noise, the harder the message is to pick up. We are all transmitting even though we are not generally aware of it.
[254] When we heat water its structure changes – this new structure is steam.

could *'move too fast to be measured'* in a *'moment too short to be measured'*, from one place to another without going through the space between, faster than the speed of light[255] then we would be taking matter instantaneously from one place to another – leaving behind the concept of time and space entirely.[256]

***

In *Astral Projection* the spirit releases itself of its physical body. For this to happen you need to relax and enter a meditative state (*See* Appendix VII) and imagine your spirit rising from your body. Traditionally the soul is believed to be attached to the physical body by a silver cord.[257] This means that the spirit will always return. The cord cannot be broken (it is a visualisation).[258] It is believed that on the journey throughout the *'astral plains'* we meet entities[259] – personifications of things within our own psyche – these are the *'demons'* locked up in our subconscious minds. These are the myths and legends the ancient Shaman brought back from their dream quests.

---

[255] In the click of your fingers light can travel to America and back 30 times.
[256] And time and space is only a man-made concept. As we have seen, time and space are beyond explanation because they cannot be explained as physical properties – they are beyond the three-dimensional world we live in – and therefore have no physical properties.
[257] Coincidentally, silver is an excellent conductor of electromagnetic energy.
[258] The superstition of not being able to return back to your body or *'losing your soul'* is a nonsense. As we have seen, this exercise is one of mental *'projection'* and, like a slide in a projector, the slide does not go anywhere.
[259] It is said that *The Astral Plain* is made up of nine upper levels – *The Higher*: believed to consist of the Feminine, Masculine, Planetary and Spiritual. *The Lower*: made up of Air, Fire, Water and Earth. And the Parallel Earth Plain. Below the Earth are two levels – The Underworld and The Void.

Appendix VII: Dream Magic

Magic is seen, by some, as the science of using emotional energy to effect a change in other energy patterns.[260] Rituals are used to build-up and discharge this emotional energy. In the creation of a curse you *'collect'* hate in your body and *'target'* it at the recipient of the curse. To help do this you gather together things *'associated'* with your target to helps focus your energy[261] – by creating a good mental image of your victim. Using incantations, visual images and incense to become totally immersed in the curse, bombarding the senses and intensifying the energy you wish to transmit. The same thing can apply to any spell. In the case of lust or love visualisation is the means of creating the energy you wish to use.[262]

In *Dream Magic* you can use the same strategies. Herbs that help dreaming are lavender, heather, peppermint, dill, sage, mugwort, elder and laurel.[263] Semi-precious stones, such as crystal, opal, topaz, turquoise and jade are also said to assist in the dream process.

The best time for *Dream Magic* is said to be during a new moon, full moon, and dark moon – when the planet passes through the astrological signs of Pisces, Cancer, Scorpio, Libra, Gemini and Leo. Each of these *'moon-seasons'* last about 60 hours – as the moon passes through the zodiac once a month. Days associated with good dreaming are:

St Agnes' Day	21st January
Imbolc	1st February
Candlemas Day	2nd February
St Valentine's Eve	13th February

---

[260] Altering the electrochemical balance of the metabolism – used in creating the body's energy.
[261] This can be things like items of clothing or photographs. In witchcraft and voodoo effigies are created in wax or clay, infused with hair and nail-clippings, to represent the recipient of the curse.
[262] Positive Visualisation is used by many high achievers – including businessmen and athletes – who claim the process helps to focus their mind on success and achieving their goals.
[263] The herbs vervain and white deadnettle are said to banish nightmares.

Lady Day	25th March
Good Friday	The Friday Before Easter
St George's Eve	22nd April
St Mark's Eve	25th April
Walpurgis Night	May Eve
May Day	1st May
Last Night of May	31st May
Midsummer Eve	23rd June
Lammas	1st August
St Faith's Day	6th October
Halloween	31st October
Samhain	1st November
Christmas Eve	24th December
New Year's Eve	31st December

The best hours to perform *Dream Magic* are between 7 and 8 in the morning, 11 and 12 midnight,[264] 5 and 6 in morning and 9 and 10 in evening.[265] The hour before dawn, and the hour after sunrise, are also thought to be good.[266]

***

Freud called dreams the *'gateway to the subconscious'*.[267] It is during sleep that the brain revises and reorganises its programmes, so that they are kept synchronised and relevant for our day to day living. Dreams occur after the first two hours of sleep. This type of sleep is called R.E.M (Rapid Eye Movement) sleep.[268] If you wake in the middle of a dream you will be able to recall it. After five minutes of waking the dream will appear hazy; after ten minutes the memory of your dream will be gone.

---

[264] Known as the *Merlin's Hour*.
[265] Known as the *Luna Hour*.
[266] After 12 noon bad dreams happen as the *'daylight demons'* appear (according to Tibetan mythology).
[267] **Sigmund Freud** *(1856–1939)* was the Viennese doctor who founded the study of psychoanalysis. His book *The Interpretation of Dreams* was published in 1900 and claimed that dreams unlock the secrets of the subconscious mind. Freud is said to have had a relationship with the German ear, nose and throat specialist Dr Wilhelm Fliess.
[268] Because the eye can be seen to move under the eyelid.

***

To create *Dream Magic,* you need to be totally relaxed. Focus on your incoming and outgoing breath. Soothe away the tension in your body and visualise what it is you wish to achieve. If it involves contacting a person call them by name in your head. Picture them as *'real'* as possible. If your wish is to heal them, *'see'* the person being healed by the energy from the heart. If it is to give them a message call that message to them in your head and visualise them receiving the message. *Dream Magic* works by the power of your thought and *'will'* to communicate.

Appendix VIII: Dionysus

Ecstasis[269] means *'to being taken out of yourself'* – to be in a profoundly altered state of being.

Through the worship of Dionysus,[270] those involved in his cult, believed themselves to be possessed by him when they reached this frenzied state. Dionysus symbolised freedom and spontaneity. He was god of dance, wine and music – later known by the ancient Romans as Bacchus[271] – he was a god of many different forms[272] and had a huge influence on Athenian culture.[273]

Dionysus was often depicted wearing animal skins,[274] he was a tree god, a bull god, and god of fertility.[275] His attendants were the *satyrs*,[276] and the women followers of his cult, named the Maenads.[277] Dionysus was sexually ambiguous, often appearing

---

[269] Meaning ecstasy.
[270] Dionysus was the slim, sensuous, and youthful deity of vegetation.
[271] And depicted by Rubens as the fat and jolly Roman god of wine.
[272] Feared and loved – always a twin image of contradictions.
[273] Dionysus was the polar opposite to the god Apollo who represented stillness and order.
[274] Dionysus is often depicted with feminine features, wearing women's clothes and sporting long hair. He is usually dressed in a fawn skin and bedecked in ivy. In his hand he carries a *thyrsus* - a blunt spear covered in ivy and crowned with a pine cone and two ribbons.
[275] Other names of Dionysus include: *"the roaring one"*, the *"bull-horned god"*, Bromios and Enorches - *"the betesticled"*. He was also the supreme deity Dimetor - *"twice-born"*, Arsenothelys - *"the man-womanly"*, Endendros - *"he in the tree"*, Omadios - *"eater of raw flesh"* and Mystes - *"the initiated"*.
[276] Half-human, half-animal. They were sexual beings, often depicted with erect penises. The name *satyr* giving us the word *'satire'* – something that is held up to scorn by ridicule.
[277] Also known as the Bacchae.

more feminine than masculine.[278] He was often associated with death and rebirth,[279] the bringer of madness, anarchy and revolution. He was the god of masquerade and the *'maker of magic'*.[280] As god of possession he would induce his followers to see the world as it was not, and his rites (like the god himself) took many forms (but always involving sexual abandon and trance). For Dionysus was capable of revealing himself directly to his followers, who were possessed by him when submerged in trance.

The Dionysiac rites took the form of an *orgy*, which just means *'a secret rite or an act of devotion'*, its sexual connotation coming much later (because of Dionysus). At midwinter the Maenads, left their homes for the wooded hillsides of Mount Cythaeron in search of communion with Dionysus – and to achieve a state of *ecstasis*. These communions involved dancing themselves into a trance-like state and ended with the tearing and eating of the raw flesh of an animal, usually a fawn, a lion, a lynx, or a bull.[281] The animal, dressed to represent the god, was believed to be the incarnation of Dionysus, so that when it was eaten they were in fact eating him.[282] Possessed by the god, they lost themselves. To the ancient Greeks, Dionysus was god of licence,[283] and unlike most sacred rituals that depend on exact repetition, the Dionysiac rites were spontaneous and individual. Later these rituals would develop into month long ceremonies called *Dionysia*,[284] where women, dressed as men,[285] paraded huge Phalluses through the streets of the City in praise of

---

[278] Dionysus is linked to male relationships with Achilles, Acoetes, Adonis, Ampelus, Hermaphroditus, Hymenaeus, Laonis and Priapus. The most notable is that with Polymnus, whom he is said to have loved. When Polymnus died, Dionysus carved a wooden phallus from a fig tree and used it in remembrance of his dead lover.
[279] He represented our *'life force'* – which is neither good or bad – it simply exists, with a potential for great love as well as an equal potential for great cruelty – just as life itself has.
[280] He was also seen as the god of inspiration.
[281] Originally it would have been a human sacrifice.
[282] This idea of taking the god into the body can also be seen in the Christian Communion of eating bread as the body of Christ. Christ was also seen as both man and god, and a resurrection deity.
[283] The followers of Dionysus placed themselves literally outside society.
[284] Beginning at the end of March.
[285] A practice banned by the Laws of Moses within the Jewish religion.

Dionysus.[286] Once in the temple, the Phallus would be covered with garlands, representing the beginning of spring, and the gift of fertility and harvest. These sacred rites give rise to songs in praise of Dionysus – songs that developed into choral epics, which later gave birth to the first known dramas[287] written by the Orphic priests – in a play seen only by the initiates of the Orphic Order. At the climax of the play the actor portraying Dionysus would be seen torn to pieces and eaten.

Dionysus, and his worship, was adopted by the ancient Romans until 186 BC, when the Roman Senate passed laws banning the worship of Dionysus – replacing it with the Roman equivalent, Bacchus, the god of wine.

***

The myth of Dionysus tells how Zeus[288] slept with a mortal woman, Semele,[289] the daughter of Cadmus, King of Thebes. But when Agave, Semele's sister heard about the affair she was jealous and tricked Semele into believing that the father of her unborn child may not be Zeus, but a mortal.[290] Worried by the thought of having an illegitimate child to a common mortal, Semele, makes Zeus promise to visit her next time *'in all his splendours, such as he wears in heaven'*, which he does, and Semele is burnt to ashes by the sight of him. Zeus, seeing what he had done, takes the child and hides him in

---

[286] A similar ritual can be found in Ancient Egypt in praise of Osiris, a resurrection god of the Pharaohs.

[287] Originally danced around the threshing floor after the last harvest was made. In Britain corn-dollies were made from the last sheaf of corn and buried in the field to thank the gods for a good harvest (originally this corn-dolly would have been a human sacrifice, maybe of a child).

[288] Ruler of the ancient Greek gods.

[289] Some of the legends start with Zagerus Dionysus, the illegitimate son of Zeus and Peresphone (Peresphone was Zeus' illegitimate daughter by the goddess Rhea) who, as a child was kidnapped by the Titans (the giant gods of Creation) who tore him to pieces and ate him. However, the goddess Athena managed to save the child's heart so that he could be born again. In revenge Zeus blasted the Titans with a thunderbolt, and it was from their remains the human race was formed.

[290] In some versions of the story the jealous woman is Hera (Zeus' wife) who visits Semele in the form of Beroe (Semele's aged nurse).

his thigh, away from Hera. Thus, Dionysus emerged as a god, twice born – once from a mortal and then again from a god. This made him unique as god and as human, causing him to be persecuted by mortals and by the gods.

Dionysus is given over to the Muses to be educated. During this time, he learns how to make wine and Zeus is forced to cast him out of Olympus. He is sent mad and left to wonder by himself alone. The goddess Rhea, however, takes pity on him, cures his madness and teaches him her sacred rites. Dionysus takes these rites from Phrygia into Asia and finally to his birthplace of Thebes.[291] All those that did not worship him he drove to madness and murder. The religion *(thought to have originated in Thrace)* is a historical fact and gives a historical basis to the worship of Dionysus – making it more than just another Greek myth.

---

[291] Where he took revenge for his mother's death – as told in Euripides' play, *The Bacchae* – the account of how Dionysus has his own cousin, Pentheus, torn apart by the Bacchae (lead by Pentheus' own mother, Agave) for trying to oppress his sacred rites in Thebes. In another story, Dionysus has Orpheus torn apart for neglecting to worship him (some believe that Orpheus and Dionysus are one in the same – thus Dionysus offers himself up to himself for sacrifice – as did Odin and Christ).

Appendix IX: Ecstasy

Ecstasy[292] is the *'street'* name of the psychedelic amphetamine *3,4-methylenedioxy-N-methamphetamine* (MDMA). A synthetic chemical derived from the oil of the sassafras tree. It was originally created by Merck Pharmaceuticals, in Germany, in 1912 and has gained huge popularity as a *'dance drug'* on the club scene since the early 8eighties Taken in the form of a pressed pill[293] (usually bearing a symbol of some description) the effects create a feeling of euphoria, openness and love. Users also report how much more intense music sounds under the influence of ecstasy.

It takes approximately 30 minutes to an hour to take effect,[294] depending on the strength of the pill and what you have taken. The effects are physically manifested in a rise in body temperature, visual distortion and jaw clenching.[295] The *'up'* feeling can last anything from 3 to 4 hours.[296]

The *'come down'* from a pill takes approximately 24 hours[297] to wear-off and leaves you feeling drained and *'hung-over'*.

Ecstasy is a Class A drug and it is illegal to poses it[298] or sell it.[299] Pills are notorious for unreliability, more than any other street drug, Ecstasy can contain anything from caffeine to amphetamines. It is unwise to combine MDMA with other drugs, and those suffering

---

[292] *'E'* or *'pills'*. (*See* Appendix VIII).
[293] Containing between 80-150mg of MDMA (at a cost of £5 per pill).
[294] It can take up to two hours to take effect sometimes.
[295] In some cases, nausea, vomiting, and dizziness.
[296] And can have a residual effect lasting up to 6 hours – which can affect sleep.
[297] Some people notice a mood shift for several days after.
[298] Carrying a prison sentence of up to 7 years for possession.
[299] Carrying a possible life sentence.

from a heart condition or high blood pressure are advised not to take it.

The long-term effects of Ecstasy are still unknown. Although not physically addictive, the drug, like any other is psychologically additive and the advice given is to limit usage to no more than once a month. This avoids the accumulation of the drug in your system that can, with over-usage, create longer periods of *'come-down'* due to the need for increased dosage in order to achieve the required *'high'*.

Dehydration is the greatest risk for Ecstasy users and can be fatal. Users are advised to drink water and take breaks[300] regularly as constant dancing increases the loss of body fluids.[301] Alcohol also dehydrates the system and is a definite non-mixer with MDMA.

If MDMA causes a panic attack the best way to deal with this is to keep calm, do not fight the feelings, but go somewhere comfortable and quiet, and talk through your anxiety with a friend. Always tell someone what you have taken and never over exceed the basic dosage of a substance you have never taken before. Remember, street drugs are not controlled, never reliable and are illegal.

---

[300] Known as *'chill out'*.
[301] However, too much fluid can cause the body to *'drown'* so do not over compensate for fluid loss by drinking too much water.

Appendix X: Ketamine

Ketamine hydrochloride is a synthetic chemical commonly referred to as a *'dissociative anaesthetic'*. Originally developed, in 1962 by Calvin Stevens, as a veterinary anaesthesiology called *CI581*.

Recreationally ketamine[302] is snorted in lines, in the form of white powder[303] – like cocaine – and takes between 5 and 15 minutes to have an effect.[304]

Used as a *'chill out'* drug after clubbing, to counter-act the effects of *Ecstasy* or *Speed*,[305] ketamine gives the user a feeling of mild drunkenness[306] and a sense of dreaminess. Other effects are the feeling of the limbs being heavy and movements therefore becoming clumsier. As a *'chill out'* drug it creates a sense of sociability and a changed perspective on the world. Users feel a delayed reaction to physical sensations and may even experience a touch of vertigo.[307]

The effects of the drug can last anywhere from between one to three hours, depending on the ketamine's strength and your tolerance levels.[308] In higher doses[309] users enter a state of complete

---

[302] Known a '*K*'.
[303] First tried for this purpose by Edward Domino who created the phrase *'dissociative anaesthetic'*.
[304] It is sold in grams at £35 per bag. Although *split-bags* of ½ grams can be bought for £25.
[305] Amphetamines –commonly known as *'uppers'* – which waken you *up* and give you energy.
[306] And a dry mouth.
[307] Some people feel nausea taking Ketamine and it can make them vomit, which can be dangerous when dealing with an anaesthetic or sedative-based drug (for obvious reasons).
[308] The body develops a quick tolerance to Ketamine that never diminishes – so users have to increase dose each time in order to get the desired effects.
[309] Known as a *K-hole*.

dissociation, entering other realities and experiencing almost *'near-death experiences'*, visions and black outs.[310]

Ketamine is one of the most psychologically addictive recreational drugs on the club scene and has the potential to become physically addictive. Regular users experience paranoia and egocentrism, and it can take a number of days to get over the drug's residual effects of drowsiness.

As with all drugs, if you take ketamine, make sure you are in a safe environment and have friends around you. Keep away from candles and machinery. Do not drive or put yourself in any situation where balance or spatial awareness are tested. Ketamine is a dangerous drug if not treated with respect.

Although possessing ketamine is not illegal, supplying it without prescription is.

---

[310] Regular users also begin to see coincidences and synchronicities in their everyday lives.

Appendix XI: *The Bible* in Context

The Bible is the Christian's sacred book comprising the *Old Testament* (a collection of writings forming the Jewish scriptures) and the *New Testament* (based on the life of Christ and the formation of the early Roman Church).

The Bible we have is from ninth and tenth century Medieval texts which have been distorted through translations from the original Hebrew into Greek, and then - finally, via Latin - into English.

Our *New Testament* is based, in part, on the writings of the Essenes *(a group of Jewish religious fanatics that lived near Qumran, by the Dead Sea)*. *Mark's Gospel* was written in Rome, for the Romans between 66-74AD under the direction of St. Paul. *Luke's Gospel* was also written for the Romans, and was probably commissioned by a high-ranking Roman official around 80AD. *Matthew's Gospel* was copied from *Mark's Gospel (but not by the disciple himself)* in around 85AD. And, finally, *John's Gospel* was written in 100AD, near the Greek city of Ephesus, and like *Matthew's Gospel* it was not written by John.

During the Dark Ages the Church managed to obscure its history *(seeing as they had a monopoly on writing it)* and in the process lost, destroyed and censored most of its activities during this very crucial period of Christian development. It is during this period that our *Bible* was created.

So *The Bible* is a collection of selected works. Other gospels and scriptures do exist. Some books have been deliberately excluded. In 367AD the first list of books for *The Bible* was created by Bishop Athanasius of Alexandria. In 393AD the list was ratified by the Church Council of Hippo, and in 397AD the Council of Carthage agreed on the final selection, *(after drastic editing, censorship and revision by Bishop Clement of Alexandria)*.

In all *The Bible* contains only seven *presumed* references to *'gay men'*:

"Thou shalt not lie with mankind, as with womankind: it is abomination."[311]

Leviticus 18:22

"If a man also lie with mankind, as he lieth with a woman, both of them have committed an abomination: they shall surely be put to death; their blood shall be upon them"

Leviticus 20:13

"There shall be no whore[312] *of the daughters of Israel, nor a sodomite*[313] *of the sons of Israel."*

Deuteronomy 23:17

"And there was also sodomites in the land: and they did according to all the abominations of the nations which the Lord cast out before the children of Israel."

I Kings 14:24

"For this cause God gave them up unto vile affections: for even their women did change the natural use into that which is against nature: And likewise also the men, leaving the natural use of the woman, burned in their lust one towards another; men with men working

---

[311] However, men who *'lie with'* men, but not as they would with *'womankind'* must be acceptable, as it is not mentioned. Therefore, it is the *how* you have sex with a man that is the *'abomination'* and not the sexual act itself. In this instance *The Bible* is teaching us to honour the gender of our partner and respect the nature of their sexuality, and their sexual needs.

[312] This is a demarcation between the Jewish religion and other religions that used sacred sexual rites with Priestesses, often referred to as Temple Prostitutes.

[313] Sodomites are the inhabitants of Sodom, referred to in *The Book of Genesis* (18–19). Sodom was the home of the Canaanite religion. The Canaanites were an early Christian sect whose teachings – although Christian – differed from the Church we have come to know today. One of these Canaanite practises involved anointing and baptising its followers with sperm or other body fluids.

that which is unseemly, and receiving in themselves that recompense of their error which was meet."

Romans 1:26–27

"Know ye not that the unrighteous shall not inherit the kingdom of God? Be not deceived: neither fornicators, nor idolaters, nor adulterers, no effeminate, nor abusers of themselves with mankind, Nor thieves, nor covetous, nor drunkards, nor revilers, nor extortioners shall inherit the kingdom of God."

Corinthians 6:9–10

"Knowing this, that the law is not made for a righteous man, but for the lawless and disobedient, for the ungodly and for sinners, for unholy and profane, for murderers of fathers and murderers of mothers, for manslayers, For whoremongers, for them that defile themselves with mankind, for menstealers, for liars, for perjured persons, and if there be any other thing that is contrary to sound doctrine."

I Timothy 1:9–10

The word *'homosexual'* does not exist in any *Bible* text because it was not created until 1869 – and its appearance in our *Bible* is only there because of the translator's imposition and interpretation. Of course, this is old news, actions can be condemned without being specifically named. But was homosexuality really being condemned?

In the second century BC – *when the first books of the Old Testament were being written* – the Israelites needed to separate themselves, religiously, from the Canaanites, who had inhabited the land before their arrival *(around 1250BC)*. Now the Canaanites used to perform sexual rituals with cult prostitutes *(as the Mesopotamians and Egyptians had done before them)*, the Jewish religion did not. After a 300-year battle with the Canaanites, the Jews had all but succeed in wiping out their adversaries by around 600BC. As the struggle with the Canaanites lessened, so did the hostility towards religious prostitution and sexual practices.[314]

---

[314] A point of fact: Pope John XII *(937–964)* was a bisexual and ran a brothel from St Peter's, as did Pope Julius II at the beginning of the 16th century.

The story of Sodom is, if you read it properly, more about inhospitability towards Abraham and the angels than about anal penetration.

If we look at this in context. In none of the Ten Commandments does it say anything about being gay, what it does say though is:

"The woman shall not wear that which pertaineth unto a man, neither shall a man put on a woman's garment; for all that do so are abominations unto the Lord thy God."
Deuteronomy 22:5

"Ye shall not round the corners of your heads, neither shalt thou mar the corners of thy beard."
Leviticus 19

It also says that children should be born inside marriage, and their paternity assured, adulterers should be put to death and brides who cannot prove their virginity might be stoned to death. The Catholic Church also made it illegal to have sex on Sundays, Wednesdays and Fridays, for forty days before Easter and forty days before Christmas *(and for three days before communion)*.

"He that is without sin among you, let him first cast a stone."
John 8:7

In the *Old Testament* the prophets say that the *'inside'* is more important than the *'external'* fulfilment of the law, because without that internal goodness *(irrespective of your acts)* it is all worthless. As with the tale of Sodom, it is not the act that is a sin, it is the way that act is committed that is sinful. Maybe modern-day Christians should read *Peter* chapter 4, verses 8–9, *'And above all things have fervent charity among yourselves; for charity shall cover the multitude of sins. Use hospitality one to another without grudging'*.

Jesus told his followers, *'behold, the kingdom of God is within you'* (Luke 17:21) and that *'A new commandment I give unto you, That ye love one another; as I have loved you, that ye also love one another.*

By this shall all men know that ye are my disciples, if ye have love one to another.' (John 13:34-35). And 'If ye keep my commandments, ye shall abide in my love; even as I have kept my Father's commandments, and abide in his love. These things I have spoken unto you, that my joy might remain in you, and that your joy might be full. This is my commandment, That ye love one another, as I have loved you. Greater love hath no man than this, that a man lay down his life for his friends.' (John 15:10–13).

Note that Jesus followed *his* Father's commandments as a Jew, as Christians we are to follow only one commandment - to love one another *(it covers all the others in a more user-friendly sort of way)*. *'Beloved, let us love one another; for love is of God; and every one that loveth is born of God, and knoweth God. He that loveth not knoweth not God; for God is love' (I John 4:7–8).*[315]

Jesus is seen as a role model. If we emulate Him we too can become at one with God. As Moses *(of the Old Testament and Jewish/Muslim faith)* erected a barrier between the sacred and the mundane – *dividing the world into the permissible and the forbidden* – Jesus broke it down and made it accessible to all Jewish and Gentile *(that means non-Jewish)*. He let us know God within ourselves, without mediation *(why do you think the Jewish priests crucified him? If religion caught on Jesus-style the priests would lose their power)*. Yet Christ's resurrection was a symbolic resuscitation of a dead religious idea – theology did the rest and used him.

Jesus and the gay community are more linked than the Christian Church would ever like to admit. So was Jesus gay? As Clement of Alexandria, in the second century said, *'Not everything that is true needs necessarily to be divulged to all men...'*

---

[315] And continues for another thirteen chapters.

Notes

A New Age of Machines

We are entering a new age of machines. A world in which we can be free of the physical ties of our human bodies. A world in which we can exist almost as a figment of our own imagination.

This is the dawn of *virtual reality*[316]. A world that is computer-generated, where reality can be simulated. A reality where the human body can experience artificially generated data as though it were real. A c*yberspace*[317] where a data matrix can be transformed into a living landscape. A place where we can live out a life, free from the boundaries of this one.

When we log-on to a network our individuality is reduced to an anonymous entry into a colossal and faceless matrix[318] – a consequence-free *'play-zone'* which allows us to express an alternative self, opening up our fantasies and allowing us to play out our dreams in the privacy of a database.

In this virtual world our fantasies can become more intense, can turn into addictive obsessions (if we let them) as we bring them into our reality. The virtual space can become our escape, a refuge into which we can withdraw – as a space of freedom – our very own mythical *Giai*.[319]

This virtual world of cyberspace is a world beyond rules; where we can explore the fluid and contextual nature of ourselves. Where we can construct and re-construct our identities without the cultural

---

[316] A term coined by Jaron Lanier in the late 1980s.
[317] *Cyberspace* is not actually a real space – it does not pre-exist the individuals who inhabit it; it comes into being by them, and by their interaction. Its status as *space* is that of potential – one of concept rather than one of geography.
[318] Bringing with it a new age of surveillance.
[319] A place of rest amidst chaos.

constraints of our minds and physical limitations. The computer allows us to transcend the body's imperfections and flaws; it allows our minds to pursue objectives without physical restraint. We leave the flesh behind and shed all that goes with it – all that defines us in terms of race, class, status, and gender – in a virtual universe where we are not affected by the bounds of our cultural baggage; a place where we can construct a *'stand-in body'* that reveals only what we want to reveal about ourselves.

In cyber-culture the body is a fluid entity. A form that lacks clear boundaries. A form that is vulnerable. It is a culture of self-reinvention where the body becomes a commodity. In the realm of *Biotechnology* we can see a trade in body parts and genetic material, where surgery can enhance and re-modify, and where the human form becomes little more than a living doll, or an aesthetic vessel to be decorated. Where *'body art'* and style become addictions of augmentation, in a consumer driven society, in pursuit of physical perfection - where we are reduced to little more than a mass-produced shell. An object – a commodified body to be bought and sold.

In a world, where the form is merely an assemblage of commodified parts, where we can fabricate individuals, the body becomes devoid of its owner. But in cyberspace our *idoru*[320] - our personal-construct, our *'synthespian'*, an homunculus[321] that lives in virtual space and becomes an object of our erotic desires - *'a thought made flesh'* - giving form to our self and to our fantasies.

As the TV screen becomes our eyes, the mobile phone our ears and voice – our brain becomes a vast computer network, with a nervous system that stretches across the globe – we have broken the barrier of our physical bodies. The death of the physical body, as who we are, is here. Reality is an illusion – a consensual hallucination that is no more real than the virtual world we construct. Our human bodies – no more real than the *idoru* we invent.

---

[320] A constructed figure in cyberspace.
[321] **Homunculus** – a magically produced human (usually miniature).

Buddhism[322] sees the *'human being as part of the whole, called the universe'* and uses meditation to lose what *'limits us by time and space'*, allowing us to *'experience ourselves'* – our thoughts and feelings – and learn how to become *'separated'* from this world. A world that is merely an *'optical delusion of our consciousness'* – a delusion which imprisons and restricts us to our *personal* desires, stopping us from *'widening our circle of compassion'*.[323]

And so this new age of machines heralds the dawn of a new age of spirituality. As the computer demonstrates the scientific reasoning behind the age-old concept of the body as a vessel.

Religion tells us we are all spirits[324] who possess an earthly body – a physical vehicle we inhabit in order to experience life on this plain of existence. If we believe that the body is *'only truly who we are'* then we will be compelled to search outside ourselves for that missing, elusive, *'something'* which will satisfy our restlessness,[325] as though living somehow restricts us in exploring the full potential of who we are and what we can experience.

When we see the void as spiritual, we try to fill it with religion. This tends to mean looking to someone, who we believe to have some sort of authority on the subject. When we look to the priest as the intermediary between us and our belief, we give away our responsibility to them and our personal connection with our own

---

[322] Founded by Siddhartha Gautama, the Buddha (or *'Enlightened One'*), nearly 2,500 years ago.

[323] Buddhism is the quest for *Enlightenment*. The Buddha says that *Enlightenment* consists of four Truths: 1) that individual existence is painful, 2) that pain stems from the attachment to worldly things, which are ephemeral, 3) that happiness can be achieved by detaching oneself from material things and 4) that *Nirvana* (egoless bliss) can be achieved by following the *Noble Eightfold Way* (right views, right intention, right speech, right action, right livelihood, right effort, right mindfulness, and right concentration).

[324] Or souls.

[325] In a material world we look for satisfaction in our jobs, in the possession of a new home or car, in our relationships with other person (who become little more than objects in our life). This pursuit of goals – and of betterment – striving continually to move beyond who and what we are.

spirituality. This is about taking back ownership. This is about becoming your own mediator. This is about setting your spirit free...

Aleister Crowley

Aleister Crowley[326] is probably the twentieth century's most famous occultist.[327] He was born, Edward Alexander Crowley,[328] and raised in a wealthy, but very strict, religious household.[329] He was taught that God punished the *'sins of the flesh'* in the *'fires of Hell'*. And it was this type of rhetoric that Crowley rebelled against.

As a child, Crowley was mischievous.[330] He made his own fireworks, which nearly killed him, and tortured a cat to see if it really did have nine lives. At the age of 14 he lost his virginity to the maid,[331] which marked the beginning of Crowley's sex life. At 17, he contracted gonorrhoea after sleeping with a prostitute and was expelled from school again.

In 1895, Crowley attended Trinity College, Cambridge, where he lived like an aristocrat, taking up climbing, rowing, poetry[332] and a great deal of sex.[333] A year later,[334] once his father's legacy had matured, he dropped out of university and went on a climbing holiday to Switzerland.

---

[326] Born on 12th October, 1875.
[327] Crowley was one of the first people to put together the disparate occult practises of different cultures to create a modern magick. He used the word *'magick'* to distinguish *'the Science of the Magi from all its counterfeits'*. The six-letter word is balanced against the five points of the pentagram, giving the magickal number of 11 as the great number of magick, or energy tending to change. K is also the 11th letter in the alphabet and the initial of *'kteis'*, the phallus.
[328] He changed his name to Aleister so that he would not have his father's name (his father was Edward Crowley).
[329] A puritanical Christian sect called the Plymouth Brethren.
[330] He was expelled from many schools.
[331] To punish his mother.
[332] Most of it sexually explicit.
[333] With both sexes.
[334] 7th December, 1896.

In November 1898, at the age 23, Crowley was initiated[335] into the *Order of the Golden Dawn*. The Hermetic Order of the Golden Dawn was founded by Dr Woodford and Dr Wynn Westcott in 1888. Their rituals were created from an old occult manuscript written by S. L. Mathers[336] He put together rituals and knowledge from lots of different sources into a logical practise of occult. His aim was to use light, colour, sound and ceremony, to train the human mind and enable it to reach its full potential.

Master of the London Temple was poet W. B. Yeats. Other members included the Astronomer Royal of Scotland, Sir Gerald Kelly, President of the Royal Academy, the writer Bram Stoker and poet Algernon Swinburne.

Crowley quickly advanced through the ranks of the Order[337] and in 1900, obtained the rank of *Adeptus Minor*, however the leaders of the Order disapproved of Crowley's homosexual activities and refused to acknowledge his rank. Soon after, Crowley left the Order and continued his work alone. It was during this time that he began performing the *Abra-Melin*.[338] A few weeks into the process, without much success, he met a young society lady called Rose Kelly.[339] After a torrid sexual fling they were married and the *Abra-Melin* was forgotten. For their honeymoon they travelled to Egypt. It was during this trip, in March of 1904, that Crowley had the single most important experience of his life.

Crowley and Rose Kelly were visiting the King's Chamber of the Great Pyramid. There Crowley began an occult invocation called the Goetia. Rose, who knew nothing about the occult, fell into a trance and began to chant, *'They are waiting for you'*. Crowley was sceptical about this *'trance'* she had fallen into and began to asked

---

[335] Taking the name Frater Perdurabo, which meant *'I will endure'* in Latin.
[336] Who translated and edited many classic Medieval occult text on the Tarot (the source of what we now know today on the subject).
[337] Reaching the grade of Practicus within two months.
[338] A black-magic ritual (taking six months to complete) dating from the 14th century, which allowed a person to have communications with their Holy Guardian Angel.
[339] Rose was later revealed to be clairvoyant.

her a series of questions, which she answered with great accuracy.[340] As if this was not proof enough, while walking around The Boulak Museum, in Cairo, she pointed across the room to a stele,[341] which could not be seen from where they stood. When they looked the stele, it was found to be painted with the image of Horus, and labelled as item number 666 in the museum's catalogue.[342] Rose went on to tell Crowley that he had offended the Egyptian god Horus by not concluding the *Abra-Melin*, a ritual he had been working on before his trip.

In his hotel room, for three days,[343] between the hour of midday and 1pm, Crowley was visited by a tall, dark figure of a man suspended in a cloud. Crowley described him as being in his thirties, *'well knit'*, with the *'face of a savage king'*. The spirit introduced himself as Aiwass,[344] messenger of Hoor-Paar-Kraat.[345] And as *The Holy Guardian Angel* spoke Crowley wrote. The result was *Liber AL vel Legis – The Book of Laws*.[346]

Crowley penetrated deeper into the world of the occult, taking another lover, this time the male writer Victor Neuberg. In 1908, they travelled to Algeria to perform an occult ritual to summon up

---

[340] With the odds of getting the answers right, without prior knowledge of the questions was 21,168,000 to 1.
[341] **Stele** – a column or slab covered with an inscription.
[342] 666 is seen as the number of the Beast (Satan). See *The New Testament: Book of Revelations* (13:18).
[343] 8th, 9th and 10th April, 1904.
[344] Originally Crowley thought his messenger's name was Aivas. This was numerically 78 in the Hebrew system. The number of Mezla, the highest Sephirah of the Kabhala, and the number of cards in the Tarot deck. Then, in 1926, his messenger corrected him with the spelling of *'Aiwass'*, which is numerically 93 (although Crowley does give it the Greek spelling of *'Aiwaz'* on occasion, to give it the number 418).
[345] Also known as Set, or Shaitan, from where we derive the name Satan.
[346] The book was first published properly on 12th March, 1912. Nine months later the Balken Wars began. It was published again in September 1913. Nine months later the First World War broke out. In 1936 (nine months later) the Sino-Japanese conflict began on Marco Polo bridge outside Peking. And in 1938… Hitler began to move the wheels of a war machine that would change Europe for ever.

Chorizon, the demon of the abyss.[347] This rite is said to open the gates of hell, and Neuberg gained a number of altered states of consciousness, which Crowley called *'aethyrs'*. It left Neuberg psychologically ruined.

In 1907, Crowley had formed the *Argenteum Astrum*, the Order of the Silver Star, an occult society based on his own *Liber AL vel Legis* manuscript. The head of a German magical order called, *Order of the Templars of the Orient*, contacted Crowley and accused him of publishing the secret of their IXth degree.

The *Ordo Templi Orientis (Order of the Templars of the Orient)* were a magical order, whose philosophy was based on Eastern sexual ritual, some of it derived from Tantrism. Crowley was unaware of connections between his work and that of the Order until he join them. His sex magick was almost identical and in 1912, he became the head of the English Order, going on to become the World Head of the *Ordo Templi Orientis*, or Order of the Eastern Temple, as he further defined his own practises. Then, in 1913,[348] Crowley and Neuberg began their Paris *'Workings'*, it was during these rituals that Crowley discovered the power of sexual magick.[349]

'It is by freeing the mind from external influences, whether casual or emotional, that it obtains power to see somewhat of the truth of things… Let us determine to be masters of our minds'.

---

[347] Based on the occult work of Edward Carpenter.

[348] On the 600th anniversary of the death of Jacques de Molay, the Grand Master of the *Order of the Knight's Templar*. An Order set up in 1118 to protected pilgrims travelling to the Holy Land. They took their name form the Temple of Solomon, in Jerusalem, where they had their headquarters (on the Dome of the Rock, on the Temple Mount) and over the years became extremely wealthy as an Order. On 11th March, 1314, King Philip IV of France, under the guidance of Pope Clement V, had the master of the Order burned at the stake, on grounds of blasphemy and perverse religious practises. The Templars were disbanded (some say the Order went underground) and is believed to be the foundation of the Masonic Orders.

[349] Heterosexual magick being *'outward'* and homosexual magick being *'inward'* and transformative.

As the First World War broke, Crowley applied to the British Intelligence Service,[350] but was rejected, in turn he began supporting the Germans, with his writing, making him an outcast in Britain. Branded as a traitor he left the country, in 1920, and went to live in Cefalu, Northern Sicily, where he created the notorious Abbey of Thelema in an old farmhouse, with his new mistress, Leah Hirsig.[351]

Tales of the depraved sexual rituals that took place at the Abbey quickly began to spread, the most notorious being when a goat was sacrificed while having coitus with Leah. She, and many others, soon become mentally unbalanced by what happened at the Abbey. Their addiction to drugs, and Crowley's increasing dependence on heroin and cocaine fuelled the atmosphere at Cefalu. The end of the Abbey came when Raoul Loveday, one of Crowley's students, died after drinking the blood of a cat. His wife, Betty May, ran back England and sold her story to *The Sunday Express*. The British media immediately began calling Crowley *'the wickedest man in the world'*. The temple was disbanded and many of Crowley's former students went insane, some committing suicide. Leah Hirsig, after her life with Crowley, turned to prostitution and finally, in 1923, Mussolini, the Italian dictator, had Crowley deported.

Crowley was homeless and spent the remaining years as a wanderer, going from boarding house to boarding house, living off the favour of friends. As the years passed, he began to lose his grasp on reality.[352] He was impotent, addicted to heroine and even disillusioned with his own philosophies. In his final years, he was a sad figure of a broken man. On 1st December, 1947, at the age of 72 he died alone. He had asked for his body to be cremated and his ashes scattered to the wind. He wanted to leave no trace of his existence.

---

[350] During the Second World War Crowley was said to have originated the *'Sign of Apophis and Typhon'*, the famous *'V'* sign used by Winston Churchill, and Intelligence Officer Ian Fleming (creator of *James Bond*) suggested that Crowley interrogate the captured Nazi leader Rudolf Hess. This never happened.
[351] Known as *The Scarlet Woman*.
[352] Although he could still play a remarkable game of chess – being able to play (and win) two games at a time, visualising the chess boards in his head. He also maintained his wicked sense of humour – *luckily!*

Crowley believed himself to be the prophet of a New Aeon, and the book became the core of Crowley's teachings. In the New Aeon, the Age of Osiris would end[353] and the Age of Horus would be ushered in.[354] The sign for this New Era would be marked by the destruction of mankind, and the old religions.[355]

The three key philosophical ideas were:

> *'Do What Thou Wilt Shall Be The Whole Of The Law'*[356]

> *'Love Is The Law, Love Under Will'*[357]

> *'Every Man And Every Woman Is A Star'*[358]

---

[353] The old age was that of Osiris (the dead god who rose again; known also as Adonis, Attis, and Jesus). The new age, that of Horus, *the Crowned and Conquering Child*, would bring new ethics to mankind.

[354] The nature of Horus was *'Force and Fire'*, and this New Aeon would be marked by the collapse of humanitarianism. The first act of Horus' reign would naturally be to plunge the world into the catastrophe of a huge and ruthless war.

[355] The New Aeon began in 1904 (Anno 0) – Era Vulgaris, the Christian era would be surpassed by the Thelemic one. Before this had been two great aeons in the history of mankind, the first was that of woman (with female deities), the second of man (with phallic and bull deities) and third was that of the dying god (Jesus, Buddha and Mohammed).

[356] What the interpretation of this means in our time seems to have been deteriorated into *'do whatever you want'*, when it should have been *'doing that which your higher self dictates'*. The higher self, or *Will* is present in all of us, but in order to follow our *'Will'*, we must first know oneself, and it is this *'self knowledge'* which is at the core of Crowley's teachings.

[357] Jesus also said *'This is my commandment, That ye love one another, as I have loved you.'* (*New Testament: John 15:17*) and *'Owe no man any thing, but to love one another: for he that loveth another hath fulfilled the law.'* (*New Testament: Galations 5:13*)

[358] Humans are made up of the same basic material as stars.

Osiris

Osiris (or Oser, meaning *'lord'*), was the son of Nut[359] and Geb[360] and the brother of Aset (Isis)[361], Nebthet[362] and Set.[363] He gave the Earth its vegetation and established the seasons. He gave order to human society, and showed man how to live by the laws and religious rituals in respect of the gods. Osiris often travelled the world,[364] leaving his wife Aset to rule Egypt as his regent, to teach mankind.

Once, while Osiris was away, the jealous Set hatched a plot to kill his brother. He built a bed from cedar wood,[365] that had a lid upon it. This beautifully carved and painted box was made to Osiris' specific measurements. Then, when Osris returned home, Set held a feast in his honour and invited him to try his new gift. As soon as Osiris was

---

[359] The ancient Egyptian sky-goddess and brother of Geb.
[360] The ancient Egyptian god of earth, and brother and husband to Nut. They are often seen as twins, and make up the physical world.
[361] Also known as Eset or Isis, the wife and sister of Osiris. She had the function of being the female counterpart of Osiris' male fertility.
[362] Sister and consort of Set (her other brother) she once seduced Osiris, and gave birth to Anubis, the jackal-headed god, who protected the pharaohs' tombs from grave-robbers and weighed the hearts of the dead before judgement in the underworld.
[363] Often seen as an evil Egyptian deity.
[364] As Odin did.
[365] Cedar wood was used in the construction of the Ark of the Covenant, the receptacle for the Hebrew's Ten Commandments from God, designed by Moses - who is thought to have been a high priest or pharaoh of Egypt. Cider wood was also used in the building of the Temple of Solomon - the final resting place of the Ark of the Covenant. Legend has it that the wood was brought to Jerusalem from the Lebanon. King Solomon was the son of David (who originally acquired the building materials for the Temple - finally built by Solomon on the summit of Mount Moriah in Jerusalem). At the entrance to the Temple stood two bronze pillars called Jachin and Boaz. These pillars feature in modern Freemasonry (and are often claimed to be represented in the upright posts of *The Hanged Man* Tarot card) an organisation which is said to be related to the Knight's Templer, who were based on the site of the Temple during the Holy Crusades. The name Solomon can also be seen as the derivative of *'Sol'* – meaning *'sun'* – and *'omon'* -- from the name *'Amun'*, the Egyptian Sun-god. Thus linking, once again, early Judaism back to the religious practises of the Ancient Egyptians.

inside the bed, Set nailed the lid down.[366] He then took the box and sank it into the Nile. The river carried Osiris out to sea, and he finally came to rest in Lebanon, where the box was lodged in the roots of a myrrh-tree.[367]

Aset searched the world for the body of Osiris, and was at last, drawn to him by the scent of the myrrh-tree. Retrieving his body, she brought him back Egypt and attempted to revive him in the form of hawk, by beating her wings to fill his lungs with air. However, all that she could revive was his penis, which ejaculated the last essence of the living god into Aset's womb. Aset then fled to the Delta with the corpse, where she bore Osiris a child, the hawk-god Horus.[368] Set, somehow, stole back the body of Osiris and carved it into fourteen pieces. He scattered thirteen of them around the provinces of Egypt, and threw the fourteenth, his penis, into the Nile,[369] where it was eaten by a crab.[370]

Once more Aset searched for Osiris' body. She took the found pieces and reassembled them on the riverbank, were she washed them with perfumed oils and wrapping them with bandages, in order to revive him once again.[371] Although the process worked, the council of gods decreed that Osiris should live in the underworld, and appointed him judge of the dead.[372]

---

[366] The first coffin.
[367] Myrrh was used as an offering to the Sun-god Ra, and used during the mummification process of the pharaohs. It is often associated with Saturn and death, and was one of the three gifts brought by the Magi to the infant Christ.
[368] *See* Horus.
[369] Thus giving the river its symbolic identification with fertility.
[370] The symbol of Cancer and the female aspects of the universe such as the tides, the moon's phases and menstruation.
[371] The first mummification.
[372] Similar to Odin.

Horus the Sun

Horus was originally a Sun-god, Ra's strength made manifest.[373] His honorary titles included Harakhty[374] and Horkhentiirti.[375] He was often shown as a small child,[376] suckling at his mother's breast, gazing out with one finger in his mouth, playing with tame snakes[377] and scorpions,[378] or riding crocodiles[379] and lions.[380]

In later myths from the Nile Delta region, Horus was said to be the child of Aset and Osiris. He was conceived when Aset took the form of a hawk, and attempted to restore life to Osiris, after his brother Set had murdered him. In these stories Horus became the hawk-headed warrior-god, and his Egyptian name Har was derived from the sound of the bird's call.[381] Horus became the mediator between the two worlds, of the living and the dead, guiding souls to judgement before Osiris and protecting the pharaohs and their households.[382]

In the Delta myth-cycles Horus exacts punishment upon Set for killing his father and usurping his power on Earth. Once Horus claimed his inheritance, from the divine court, a war emerged, but Ra refused to listen. In one such battle Set found Horus hiding in the desert[383] and gouged out his eyes;[384] light disappeared from the

---

[373] As Christ was God's power manifest on Earth.
[374] *Horus of the Horizon.*
[375] *Horus of the Two Eyes.* Meaning lord of the Sun and of the Moon.
[376] Called Herupakhret - *'Horus the child'* or the Greek Harpocrates. In an image very similar to those painted of the infant Christ and his mother.
[377] The phallus image.
[378] The symbol of war (Scorpio).
[379] The symbol of Sobek, the creature that was believed to eat the hearts of the unjust in the Underworld.
[380] The symbol of strength and the sun (Leo).
[381] And since hawks represented the sky he was merged with the sun god to create a new deity, and Osiris' authority on Earth.
[382] Similar to the role of Odin in Valhalla.
[383] As Satan once found Christ.
[384] Odin also was said to have had one eye, after paying the price for the wisdom of the runes.

earth,[385] and was returned only when Hather,[386] resorted his sight. However, only one eye was resorted, the other was left rolling in the darkness, which was Set's domain, and this became the moon.[387]

The struggle for power is eventually ended when Set brings about his own downfall by raping Horus, a crime which Aset uses to Horus' advantage before the Celestial Court. Set's punishment is then metered out by Horus who rips away Set's testicles and so destroying his masculine power.

The eternal fight between Set and Horus is, in essence, the eternal fight between the powers of light and dark, good and evil, masculine and feminine. While at war these elements are balanced and in harmony. There is order. In this battle Set and Horus merge to form an indivisible union.[388] In this union Set (now emasculated) gives birth to Horus' child,[389] pictured as a golden disk on Set's forehead.[390] Thoth[391] is said to have been this child. Known as *The Son of the Two Lords* and *'Shepherd of the Anus'* it is he who gave numbers and measurements to mankind. It is he who defines learning, defined as *'the dual power in which the two gods are at peace'*.[392]

---

[385] As it did when Christ's mortal body died upon the cross.
[386] Horus' consort.
[387] The *'udjat'* was the Cult of Horus' Eye, which later became a universal symbol of good luck.
[388] Known as *Tau*, the supreme truth of the universe. The constant ebb and flow of change. In Taoism each person is a reflection of the entire universe (a microcosm within the macrocosm), with the flow of *yin* and *yang* (positive and negative energies), which is the very basis of life.
[389] A child coveted by the gods.
[390] Denoting this as a spiritual birth rather than a physical one.
[391] Thoth is the ancient Egyptian god of learning and wisdom.
[392] And so suggesting at the positive spiritual and intellectual benefits of homosexual union (echoed by Crowley and many Shamanic practices world-wide), which is in direct contrast to the Jewish, Christian and Islamic religious teachings of the modern world. What keeps us from our spirituality is nothing more than our *'presumed'* dependence on a spiritual mediator.

The Annotated *'Havamal'*

I know I hung a windswept tree,[393]
Nine long days and nights.[394]
Gashed by mine-own spear,[395]
Sacrificed to Odin,
An offering to myself.[396]
Bound to a tree that no man knows,
        whither its roots do run.[397]

None gave me bread,
Nor gave me ale.[398]
And I peered down into the deepest depths,
        and there I saw the runes,[399]
With a mighty cry I seized them up
        and fell back into myself once again.[400]

---

[393] This refers to the Great Ash Tree called *Yggdraill* (sometimes spelt *yggdrail* or *yggdrasil*), meaning *'ash-tree horse of Ygg'* or *'the world tree'*. This was believed by the Norse people to hold up the nine lays of the Universe.

[394] Nine is a reoccurring number in Norse mythology. It denotes cosmic significance and was the total number of planets in early astronomy. As the greatest prime number, it also symbolised spiritual achievement and became the number of initiation. It was believed that the number nine could control the force of nature and was linked to the mastery of *'lessons in life'* and the deeds of authority.

[395] As Christ hung on the cross his side was pierced by a spear. (*New Testament: John 19:34*)

[396] *See* Appendix I.

[397] *Yggdraill* was believed to have three roots. The longest coming from the ice well of Hvergelmir in Niflheimin, the home of the dead, the second root grew from the well of Mimir in Midgard, and was believed to be the source of all wisdom. And the third root came from the well of Urd in Asgard, home of the three Norns who tended it. The Norns were three sister (Skuld, Urd and Verdandi) who wove the tapestries of human destiny and in turn, controlled mankind's fate.

[398] Without food or drink the body's functions begin to shut down (as we begin to die). During this process the mind hallucinates and enters a dreamlike state of being, or trance. It is during this trance states that shaman and medicine men make connections with the spirit world.

[399] Runes are the prediction tools used by the ancient tribes of Northern Europe. Similar to Tarot cards, each Rune is symbolic and carries a meaning that can be interpreted, or read, within a given context. (*See* Appendix II)

As I won back my strength, wisdom thrived too,
As word leads to word, and deed to deed.
I understood my course.

Havamal[401] - *The Poetic Edda, c 1200 AD.*

---

[400] Man can survive up to 12 weeks without food, but only 11 days without sleep.
[401] Meaning *'The Voice of the High One'*.

Further Crippled

Here is a selection of other works to help continue your journey into the world of the *Cripple*.[402] Remember that some of the places on the journey are to be discovered – and some are there to be revisited – and each time we go back with new eyes we see different things...[403]

- *A Day in the Death of Joe Egg* by Peter Nichols (1967) – a stage-play (later made into a movie) exploring the strain of raising a severely disabled child.

- *God is a DJ* by Pink (2003) – from her album *Try This*.

- *A Space Odyssey* (1968) – Stanley Kubrick's classic movie, based on Arthur C. Clarkes's short story *'The Sentinel'*.

- The lithographs of graphic artist M.C. Escher – *Drawing Hands* (1948), *Relativity* (1953), *Concave and Convex* (1955), *Belvedere* (1958), *Ascending and Descending* (1960), and *Waterfall* (1961).

- *Sgt. Pepper's Lonely Hearts Club Band* by The Beatles *(1967)* – this album chanced popular music forever, turning pop into art. The whole album has a meaning for *Cripple*, but pay special attention to George Harrison's *Within You Without You*.

- *Twelve Monkeys* (1995) – Terry Gilliam's movie starring Bruce Willis and Brad Pitt.

---

[402] These works have been placed in a specific order to take you on a journey into some of the ideas and concepts explored within this book.
[403] All the website address are correct at the time of publication.

- *Mysterious Stranger* by David Blaine (2003) – published by Pan Books, London. An interesting insight into the work and influences of illusionist David Blaine.

- *Affirmation* by Savage Garden (1999) – the whole album is worth listening, but the songs *Affirmation*, *I knew I Loved You* and *Crash and Burn* are particularly relevant.

- *Orlando* by Virginia Woolf (1928) – a story of love that can cross the seas of time.

- The performance work of *Theatre de Complicite*. Information about the company can be found on their website: *www.complicite.org*.

- *Venus as a Boy* by Bjork (1993) – from her album *Debut*.

- *Eqqus* by Peter Shaffer (1973) – a stage-play (later made into a movie starring Richard Burton) about a disturbed young man and the relationship he develops with his psychiatrist.

- *The Nines* (2007) – a psychological sci-fi thriller written and directed by John August. A film broken into three chapters that centre around three men who try to uncover the secret of their strange, sometimes overlapping, lives.

- *Big Fish* (2003) – Tim Burton movie based on the novel by Daniel Wallace.

- *The Metamorphosis* by Franz Kafka (1916) – his short story *The Hunger Artist* is also relevant.

- *Ready Player One* (2018) – a sci-fi movie by Steven Spielberg about virtual reality.

- *The Matrix Trilogy* by Andy and Larry Wachowski – *The Matrix* (1999), *The Matrix Revolution* (2003) and *The Matrix Reloaded* (2003) is the conceptual tale of Thomas Anderson (Keanu

Reeves), a computer hacker in the year 1999, who discovers that his reality is nothing more than an elaborate facade. The year is 3999 and the world has been laid waste, and taken over by advanced artificial intelligence. The facade, known as The Matrix, has been created to placate the A.I.'s human host, so its life essence can be *'farmed'*. Rebel warriors Morpheus[404] (Laurence Fishburne) and Trinity[405] (Carrie Ann Moss) leads Anderson, known as Neo,[406] into the real world and his destiny.

- *A Midsummer Night's Dream* by William Shakespeare (1595) – best read in the Arden Edition, this is one of Shakespeare's most accessible works and is set in three worlds (the rustic world of the working class, the noble world of the Court and the mystical world of the Fairies). Midsummer Night has always been associated with dreams and tricks of perception. In August Strindberg's play *Miss Julie* (1888), the relationships between class and gender are explored during an encounter on a Midsummer night's eve.[407]

- *The House of Dr Dee* by Peter Ackroyd (1993) – John Dee (1527–1608), was a mathematician and astrologer[408] who, in 1581 was said to have summoned up a spirit called Uriel who gave him the power to call angels. They gave Dee a magic mirror in which he could see the future. The Mirror, made of polished crystal, presently resides in the British Museum.

---

[404] **Morpheus** – the ancient Greek god of sleep and dreams.
[405] **Trinity** – the union of God, Jesus and the Holy Spirit in one form. Three is also widely regarded as a spiritual number as it has a beginning, middle and end.
[406] **Neo** – meaning *'new'* is also an anagram of *'one'*, the symbol of unity and the number associated with God, and everything in the universe.
[407] **Midsummer**, sometimes called the Summer Solstice or Litha, meaning *'stopping of the sun'* (held on 21st or 24th June). This is the longest day of the year, a time when the sun is at its highest in the sky. The date has had spiritual significance for thousands of years – the Pagans celebrated with bonfires that would add energy to the sun and the Chinese held a festival of light to the goddess Li. For the Pagans this was the time of year when the God and Goddess had their union, resulting in the harvesting of the fields.
[408] He was also made warden of Manchester College for a time. While he was there seven people were possessed by demons, and he refused to allow them to be exorcised.

- *Transformer* by Lou Reed (1972) – an album, produced by David Bowie. Also interesting is the album *The Velvet Underground and Nico* (1967), produced by the artist Andy Warhol. Each album contains a number of tracks worth listening to.

- *Hellraiser* (1987) – Clive Barker's movie *Hellraiser* is based around a puzzle box. This puzzle – the Lamont Configuration – when solved, opens a doorway to Hell, and unleashes the Cenobites – to some they are angels, and to others they are demons – whose greatest pleasure is the greatest pain. The movie spawned a number of sequels, including: *Hellbound* (1988), *Hell on Earth* (1992), *Bloodline* (1996), *Resurrection* (2000), *Hellseeker* (2002), *Deader* (2004) and *Hellworld* (2004).

- *Not I* (1972) and *Rockaby* (1981) by Samuel Beckett – two stage-plays that investigate the essence of crippled communication.

- *Diamond Dogs* by David Bowie (1974) – from his album by the same name. This influential artist is a master of reinvention and metamorphosis.

- *Queer as Folk* (1999) – A Channel Four series, first broadcast on Tuesday, 23rd February, 1999, in eight half-hour episodes. The drama, written by Russell T. Davies, follows the lives of three gay men in Manchester's gay *Village*. Starring Aiden Gillen as Stuart Allan Jones, Craig Kelly as Vince Tyler and Charlie Hunnam as the 15-year-old Nathan Maloney.

- *The Passenger* and *Lust for Life* by Iggy Pop (1977) – from his album *Lust for Life*. The title track of this album was written with David Bowie (as were a number of other tracks on the album).

- William S. Burroughs – this amazing writer can best be appreciated in Picador's *A William Burroughs Reader*, edited and introduced by John Calder (1982) – an excellent collection of extracts spanning some of his best-known works.

- The performance work of *DV8 Physical Theatre*. Information about the company can be found on their website: *www.dv8.co.uk*

- The art work of Austrian painter Egon Schiele,[409] in particular: *Self-Portrait Nude, Facing Front* (1910), *Self-Portrait Masturbating* (1911) and *Nude Girl with Crossed Arms (Gerti)*, painted in 1910. This portrait of his nude sister has many erotic undertones, and he almost certainly had a sexual relationship with her.

Egon Schiele *(12th June, 1890 – 31st October 1918)* was an Austrian Expressionist painter[410] who examined his own sexuality in disturbing images, painted as he stood in front of his studio mirror, masturbating. His pictures depict his wide-eyed stare, giving him the look of a trapped animal. His work is a fascinating study in the physical and mental sensations of auto-eroticism.[411]

Schiele's female nudes – done in watercolour – look like *'mutilated corpses'* and feature a host of pre-pubescent girls he picked up from the slums of Vienna to pose for him.[412] On the 13th April, 1912, Schiele was arrested and charged with *'immorality'* and *'seducing a minor'*, he spent 24 days in prison and had one of his drawings burnt. A second charge related to a 13-year-old girl followed. Schiele died during an Influenza epidemic on the 31st October, 1918.

---

[409] In German *schielen* means *'to squint'*.
[410] Who had been a pupil of **Gustav Klimt** *(1862–1918)*. Klimt was born in the suburbs of Vienna and, in 1897, was a founder of the Vienna *Secession* (a Nouveau Art movement similar to Impressionism) that opposed traditional academic art. Klimt's painting, *The Kiss* (1908) – his most famous work – was symbolic of what the *Secession* stood for. When the painting was first shown – like all his work – is caused a scandal because of its display of nudity, sexuality and eroticism.
[411] He seems to have only been able to gain sexual satisfaction through masturbation.
[412] They appear unselfconscious – their expressions vacant.

- The Japanese performance work known as Butoh – an art form that began in 1959 and is based on *'the experience'* of *'the event'*. Butoh cannot be spoken because it is *'that which happens within the silences of noise, within the spaces of the world'*. For further information see *Butoh: Shades of Darkness* by Jean Viala, published by Tuttle Publishing, 1988.

- *The Holy Books of Thelema* by Aleister Crowley (1904) – published by Weiser Books, this is the definitive copy of Crowley's *Book of the Law*, as dictated to him by Aiwass in Egypt.

- *Blackstar* (2016) David Bowie's twenty-fifth and final album.

- *Ray of Light* (1998) Madonna's seventh album.

***

- For more information about the Alexander Technique can be found at: *https://alexandertechnique.co.uk/*

- *The Ultimate Gay Guide* by John Szponarski (1999) – one of the best books for information about the British *'gay scene'* with useful advice, addresses and a full guide to clubs and pubs in the British Isles.

- *www.gaydar.net* – the web address of one of the biggest and most popular gay dating sites in the country.[413]

- For more information about drugs and drug use can be found at: *dancesafe.org*.

- *Essential* music playlist: *Now I'm Free* - Stuart, *The Beat Goes On* - Bob Sinclair, *So Much Love To Give* - Together, *Shine On*

---

[413] **Note**: Always remember never to give out contact information over the internet, and if you do decide to meet up with someone you have met on a dating site, tell someone where you are going, meet in a busy public place and always make sure you keep yourself safe! Follow the site's guidelines and never put yourself in a dangerous situation.

Me - Praise Cats, *Rhythm Is A Dancer* - Snap vs Run DMC, *Keep Rising Up* - Mr Timothy, *Shiny Disco Bollox* - Hoxton Whores, *Catch The Sandstorm* - Darude vs Martha Wash, *Broken Bones* - Love Inc, *Insomnia Remix* - Faithless, *Everybody's Free* - Angel One, *Dancin* - DJ Scott, *Come With Me* - Special DJ and *Look At Me Now* - Happy Hardcore.[414]

---

[414] Music taken from the summer of 2003.

Conclusion

"We must act out passion before we can feel it"
  Jean-Paul Sartre *(1905–80)*, from his book *The Words*, 1964.

We are not a body or a brain, but reside there to experience this reality. But there are countless other realities to explore.[415] It is the ability *to* live that is important, not how, and life is only ever *truly* lived when our souls are free. Being trapped in a place, or a body, or an emotional state, is merely a concept. You can be free in the darkest prison or trapped in the vastest desert. All you have to do is see beyond the physical limitations of the concept of *this* reality.

---

[415] Virtual worlds of cyberspace and the shadow worlds of sleep and day-dreams are there to be experienced too – in different ways.

Notes

Notes

Notes

Notes

Notes

Notes

Lightning Source UK Ltd.
Milton Keynes UK
UKHW022255281020
372369UK00005B/22